MELISSA THOMSON

TITO
THE
BONECRUSHER

SQUARE
FISH

Farrar Straus Giroux

New York

SQUARE
FISH

An imprint of Macmillan Publishing Group, LLC
120 Broadway, New York, NY 10271
mackids.com

Square Fish and the Square Fish logo are trademarks of Macmillan and
are used by Farrar Straus Giroux under license from Macmillan.

Our books may be purchased in bulk for promotional, educational,
or business use. Please contact your local bookseller or the
Macmillan Corporate and Premium Sales Department
at (800) 221-7945 ext. 5442 or by email at
MacmillanSpecialMarkets@macmillan.com.

Library of Congress Control Number: 2016020105

ISBN 978-1-250-23331-8 (paperback) / ISBN 978-0-374-30356-3 (ebook)

Originally published in the United States by Farrar Straus Giroux
First Square Fish edition, 2020
Book designed by Andrew Arnold and Aimee Fleck
Square Fish logo designed by Filomena Tuosto

1   3   5   7   9   10   8   6   4   2

AR: 5.1 / LEXILE: 780L

For Charlie and Pete

CONTENTS

TITO ★ THE ★ BONECRUSHER

☆ PROLOGUE ☆

A HERO ALWAYS SAVES THE DAY

Although he was six foot five and super muscular, Bruce Paxton moved unnoticed through the shadows outside the high-security lab. For one thing, no one was around *to* notice him. Also, it was nighttime.

Paxton, who was on a mission of totally dire importance, crept alongside the back wall of the concrete building. His luchador mask, which always covered his face, was barely visible in the darkness.

"This is kind of scary, right?" I whispered to my dad, whose face was also barely visible in the darkness of the movie theater in Florida where we were watching Tito the Bonecrusher's newest movie, *Steel Cage 2: Back in the Cage*. Tito is a former pro wrestler who is famous as the highest-paid action star to never be unmasked. *Steel Cage 2* was the long-awaited sequel to *Steel Cage*, in which Tito had first played former wrestler Bruce

Paxton and launched his career as an action-movie superstar.

Dad's eyes stayed on the screen, but he nodded.

"I think this is scarier than *Steel Cage*," I added. I had to turn my whole head every time I wanted to say something to Dad. I was wearing the Tito mask that Dad had gotten me for my tenth birthday, and it didn't exactly fit anymore, so I couldn't see out of the corners of my eyes. But that was okay, because the mask still looked amazing.

"Shhh," my sister, Louisa, hissed on the other side of me.

"You shhh," I replied.

I turned my attention back to the screen, where Bruce Paxton had stopped moving. He eyed a nearby bush that was making a loud rustling sound. Someone else was out there.

Bruce Paxton knew better than to make the first move. He waited for whoever was in the bushes to reveal himself.

I held my breath.

A bunny hopped out of the bush and away into the night.

"*Whew*," I said.

"Would. You. Shut. Up. Oliver," Louisa murmured.

Dad patted my hand.

Bruce Paxton reached a door marked DELIVERIES ONLY.

He punched in an access code on the keypad. It beeped once. Then the DELIVERIES ONLY door whisked open to show a large, dimly lit concrete space.

Paxton stepped inside. "Hello?" he called into the emptiness.

No answer.

Paxton began to cross the dark room. Suddenly, the lights came on, and out of *nowhere* a MAN appeared in front of him.

"*Ahhhhh!*" I hollered.

I could feel my dad jump about six inches out of his seat beside me.

"He startled me," I whispered.

"Obviously," my dad whispered back.

Louisa sighed almost louder than I had yelled, and she got up and moved to the end of the row.

"Hey, masked man," said the guy who'd just shown up out of nowhere. He was wearing a lab coat with DR. CEREBRO, HEAD SCIENTIST embroidered on it, but we all recognized the actor as John Rancid, the United Wrestling Entertainment (UWE) wrestler who'd stolen the U.S. Champion belt two years ago, because he's one of the biggest jerks in wrestling. "You're in the wrong place. This is an important laboratory for scientific geniuses."

Paxton pretended to be confused. "Isn't this the delivery entrance?" he asked.

"Yeah," Cerebro growled. "Only we aren't expecting any deliveries at this hour."

"Oh yeah? Were you expecting this?" Paxton asked.

"Expecting what?" Cerebro said.

"This," Paxton replied as he jumped onto a stack of boxes.

Before Cerebro knew what was happening, Bruce Paxton did a springboard moonsault off the stack of boxes and landed on Cerebro.

Everyone in the theater cheered.

But that was just the beginning of the action. Cerebro had fallen into a huge pile of packing material, so he was completely unharmed. He got up and began wrestling Bruce Paxton for real. They went to the top of the boxes about ten times, knocking each other down and getting back up over and over again.

It was amazing.

"You're a cuss-word fool," Cerebro growled when Paxton had him pinned to the floor for good.

(If my parents ever hear me saying a real cuss word, I'm never allowed to watch a Tito the Bonecrusher movie again, so when I quote dialogue with cuss words I just say *cuss word*.)

"I'm a fool who's going to rescue someone from this fancy lab of yours," Paxton replied.

"Oh, really? You think you can come in here and rescue a person like some kinda cuss-word hero?" Cerebro continued as Paxton started tying his wrists together with shipping tape. "My security team will catch you. You aren't going to save the day."

"In case you hadn't noticed, Dr. Genius, it's not daytime," Paxton said. He finished with the shipping tape and stood up. "Maybe I'm not a scientist, but I'm Bruce Paxton," he proclaimed. "And Bruce Paxton always saves the day—even when it's night."

We all clapped.

The rest of the movie was just as great, and when it was over we got dessert at this place we had never been to before on any of our visits with Dad in Florida. It was called AW, SWEET!, and it had something called the Li'l Sugar Bar, which was this buffet of mini cupcakes, teeny-tiny pies, and other shrunken versions of desserts. You could put as much as you wanted on your plate, and they charged you by the weight.

"It's too bad they don't have an AW, SWEET! in Virginia," I said after we sat down with our desserts.

"See how you feel after you eat what's on your plate,

Spaghetti-O," Dad said, laughing. Dad gave me the nick-name Spaghetti-O because when I was little, I thought all the Spaghetti-Os were Os for Oliver. I used to feel sorry for Louisa that there were no Spaghetti-Ls.

Dad turned to Louisa, who never cared that there were no Spaghetti-Ls. "I know it's almost six months away, but do you know where you want to celebrate after your graduation?" he asked her.

"Not a steakhouse," Louisa said.

Dad had moved to Florida from Virginia (where Louisa and I live with our mom) to help open some new steakhouses owned by this famous restaurant guy Walker Stewart. But Dad wasn't working for the steakhouse chain anymore, because Walker Stewart turned out to be a total jerk.

"Definitely not a steakhouse," Dad said with a half smile.

"Maybe O'Connell's," Louisa said. "I don't know. I can't really think about graduation and dinner at the same time."

Louisa was going to graduate in June from Haselton High School and had to give a speech at the graduation ceremony because she was going to be valedictorian, which is the person with the best grades in the whole senior class. Or maybe salutatorian, if she came in second. It was pretty close between her and this girl Mitzy Calhoun for the top spot, and they wouldn't know until the spring. But either way, she'd be giving a speech, and Dad was super-duper proud of her and told everyone about it, even strangers.

"Do you want me to holler 'That's my daughter!' at the beginning or the end of the speech?" Dad joked.

I thought Louisa would be embarrassed, but she looked worried. "You'll be there, right?" she said.

"Of course," Dad said.

"Why wouldn't he be there?" I asked.

Louisa looked at me like my brain was empty.

"I'll be there," Dad said to Louisa.

I realized Louisa was thinking about the legal stuff. There was some issue with Mr. Stewart and a bunch of tax paperwork that the government thought Mr. Stewart had lied about. Dad couldn't leave Florida until it was all sorted out. He had to get a lawyer and go to court and everything.

"Are you sure?" Louisa said.

Dad nodded and kind of waved his hand like *Don't worry about it.* "Everything is going to be fine," he said.

"Do you promise?" Louisa pressed him.

Dad paused. He looked at me and then back at Louisa. He took her hand. "I promise," he said.

"He said he's coming, Louisa," I said. "Relax."

Louisa was always so worked up about stuff that was

no big deal. Dad hadn't done anything wrong, so as soon as he got a chance to explain that in court, he'd be able to leave Florida. He had told us it was almost figured out, and the graduation was still months away. I didn't know why Louisa was making things awkward. I focused on eating my micro-doughnuts without getting powdered sugar on my Tito mask. Dad had said it: Everything was going to be fine.

★ 1 ★
EVERYTHING WAS NOT GOING TO BE FINE

Around two months before Louisa's graduation, I found out that everything was *not* going to be fine.

It was late afternoon on a regular weekday. I was doing homework with my best friend, Brain, at her house after school. We were in the same fifth-grade class at this private school called Haselton Academy that Brain's been going to since kindergarten, but where I just started this year. Anyway, we were about to do our science assignment when I realized I'd left my workbook at home.

Brain lives three houses down from me. I used to live all the way across town before my mom married my step-dad, Carl, and we all moved in with him. Moving three houses down from Brain has been convenient for lots of reasons, including that it takes about two minutes to run home and back if I forget something.

So I ran home and up the stairs to get my science workbook from my room, figuring it wouldn't take long at all. But as I was digging around in a pile of stuff next to my desk, I heard a weird noise. It sounded like someone was laughing in the walls.

At first I thought maybe it was a ghost, and I started wondering if anyone had ever died under suspicious circumstances in Carl's house, like way back in the 1970s or something, before he even moved in.

Then it occurred to me that the sound was probably coming from Louisa's room, which didn't make sense, since she was supposed to be at her part-time job.

I went to investigate.

I got to Louisa's doorway and saw that she was face-down on her bed, laughing into her pillow, making noises like *huh, huh, huhhhh*. I had no idea what she was laughing at, but just the sound of it was funny to me. So I started laughing, too.

That made Louisa sit up and whip her head around toward the door, and that's when I saw that her face was all blotchy and her eyes were puffy and she wasn't actually laughing. She was crying. Hard.

But before I could say sorry for laughing and ask her what was wrong, her face twisted into something completely angry. She leapt off the bed and yelled, "GET OUT OF HERE!"

I took a step back when she was roaring at me, so I managed to be out of the way when she slammed the door in my face.

I didn't react at first, really. I stood there for a few seconds. Then I heard my mom calling to me.

"Oliver? Can you come here?"

I hurried down the stairs. Mom was standing in the doorway between the kitchen and the living room.

"I didn't do anything to Louisa," I started to explain. "I thought she was at work. She just started yelling at me—"

"Let's sit down," she said, and she took my hand and led me over to the couch. "Your father . . . ," she began. Then her face got all red, which meant she was trying not to cry. Mom is super, super white, so when she's trying not to cry, she looks sunburned. I wasn't too worried yet, because a lot of things make Mom cry. "Your father appeared before the judge today, and he entered a plea bargain."

"Okay," I said. That just sounded like more of the courtroom stuff we'd been hearing about for a while.

"Do you know what that means, Oliver?" she asked.

"Yeah," I said. I didn't know, really, but I didn't feel like hearing my mom describe the boring details. Plus there was something else about Mom's face that was making me nervous.

Mom grabbed both my hands and looked at me. "Your father has to serve a two-year sentence."

If someone had said that in a Tito movie, I would have understood what it meant. It meant that the character had to go to jail. But hearing my mom say it, it was like the words didn't go together. I was thinking of *sentence* like a group of words, and *serve* like serve food at a restaurant. I was thinking, *How can someone serve a sentence?* And I couldn't make sense of it. So I just sat there looking at her.

"Because the case was in Florida," Mom said, "he will be in a federal correctional center there."

"What's a correctional center?" I asked.

"It's . . . it's a prison," Mom said.

Now my brain was telling me that the thing I was hearing was not right.

"Dad's not going to prison," I said. "He's coming here to visit us in two months."

Mom shook her head.

"Yes," I insisted. "He's going to be at Louisa's graduation. He promised her."

"No, honey," Mom said, her eyes wobbly. "He's not. He pleaded guilty to a lesser charge and has to serve two years. So he can't come back. Not yet, anyway."

I stared at her, and something in my bones started to itch.

"You and Louisa can still go to visit him," she said, squeezing my hands.

"Who will pick us up from the airport?" I asked.

Mom looked surprised. I guess she hadn't thought the first question I'd ask her after she told me my dad had to go to jail would be about getting picked up from the airport.

In *Coyote Willis, Pioneer Cop*, which is one of Tito the Bonecrusher's movies, Tito plays Coyote Willis, a pioneer cop in the Wild West. Tito's former manager, The Germ, plays Cactus, who is Coyote Willis's best friend and deputy. There's a scene where Coyote Willis is trying to help this lady after her family and all of her things are taken by bandits. Instead of answering Coyote's questions about where the bandits may have gone, she keeps wailing, "I need my haaaats!" And Cactus gets furious. He says, "Stop worrying about your stupid hats! We are trying to save your family!" But Coyote Willis says, "I think she's in shock. She doesn't know what she's talking about." Then he talks to the hats lady in this serious but calm voice to get her to relax before he finds the bandits and does a corkscrew moonsault onto their villainous leader to slam him into the dust.

I think I was in shock when I first heard that Dad had to go to jail. And that's why instead of asking an obvious question, like *Why is Dad serving a sentence if Walker Stewart is the one who broke the law?* or *They can send you to jail just because your boss is a criminal?*, I asked who would pick us up at the airport.

It was still an embarrassing question, though.

"Uncle Victor will pick you up, honey," my mom said. Uncle Victor wasn't my real uncle, but he was like a brother to my dad. They basically grew up in the same house, and so when Dad moved to Florida, he got a place near Uncle Victor, who had already lived there for a while. Other than being close to the beach and going to places like AW, SWEET!, the only good thing about Dad moving to Florida was that we got to see Uncle Victor a lot more.

"Oh, okay," I said. "That makes sense."

"What other questions do you have?" Mom asked hesitantly, like my next question might be about something even less important than getting picked up at the airport.

I tried to think of more questions. But the only question in my head was *How can we make this not happen?* Somehow I knew not to ask my mom. Maybe I could ask Louisa.

"Um, I don't have any more questions right now. I just want to go back to my room."

"Are you sure?" Mom asked. "I can come with you."

"No thanks," I said. I stood, patted Mom awkwardly on the arm, and walked as fast as I could out of the living room and up the stairs.

Louisa let me into her room, but she didn't say a word.

"This is not good," I said.

No response.

"We have to do something," I added.

"There's nothing we can do," Louisa finally said. "It's final. He's going to jail, and he totally lied to us. He's such a liar."

"He didn't know!" I said.

"He had to know it was a possibility," Louisa said. "And he promised me anyway that he would come. He never should have made a promise he didn't know he could keep."

"He didn't break the law!" I said. "Why would he think he was going to jail?"

"He must have done something wrong," Louisa said. "If he lied about coming to my graduation, he probably did something wrong."

"No," I said. The only person who was wrong was Louisa. "Don't say that. We know he didn't do anything. We need to help him."

Louisa laughed at me, and not in a nice way. "You're eleven years old. You're literally the last person who could do something to help."

"You're wrong," I said.

Just then the landline rang, so I took the opportunity to get the heck out of Louisa's room. I ran into Mom and Carl's room and picked up the receiver.

It was Brain.

"Do you need help looking?" she said.

"Huh?"

"For your workbook?"

I had totally forgotten.

"Oh, I, uh . . ."

"Are you okay?" she asked.

"Not really. We kind of . . . My mom said that my dad . . . You know that paperwork and tax stuff with Walker Stewart? I guess he lost the case." Aside from Mom and Louisa, Brain was the only person I ever talked to about my dad. It's not my style to go blabbing my business to anyone who will listen.

"What does that mean?" Brain asked.

"It means they thought he was, like, guilty," I said.

"No, I mean, what happens now? Does he have to pay a fine? Does he have to serve time?"

"Uh, the second one," I said. "He's going to miss Louisa's graduation." It's funny how sometimes you don't even realize that words make pictures in your head until the pictures change. It used to be that when I said *Louisa's graduation*, I could picture myself in the hot sun with a bunch of people listening to Louisa talk about how smart she is. But when I said *Louisa's graduation* to Brain on the phone, I pictured Louisa roaring "Get out!" at me, and then telling me I was the last person who would ever be able to help.

"What are we going to do? We have to do *some*thing," Brain declared.

"I don't know," I told her. "Louisa said there's nothing we can do. She said especially not me."

"Oh my God, Spaghetti-O, that is like the total opposite of what Tito the Bonecrusher would say," Brain responded immediately.

And she was right about Tito. His catchphrase is "Never quit trying!" He started saying it because of some really sad fan letter he got from a kid, and now that he's an action star, he says it at least once in every movie. Usually when he's about to break down a door or something.

"When *everyone else* thinks we should quit trying"— Brain said the words *everyone else* like they were cuss words, because she hates being like everyone else—"that's when we *definitely* need to do something."

"Whoa. You're right," I said. "We have to do something."

"For sure," Brain said.

There was a silence.

"Like what?" I asked.

"I don't know," she said. "But we will think of something."

She sounded confident. And Brain is practically a genius, so I trust her. She's probably even smarter than I am when it comes to thinking up ideas.

"Don't tell anyone, okay?" I said to Brain before we hung up.

"Obviously," Brain replied.

And that was it. One thing I appreciate about Brain is that she doesn't try to ask me about my feelings or anything mushy like that.

After an awkward dinner with Carl and Mom that Louisa refused to join, I sat in my room thinking about what Brain and I could do. I thought maybe we could speak to the judge directly, or wiretap Walker Stewart, my dad's former boss, in case he confessed that he was the one who did the illegal stuff, not my dad.

The phone rang again. I figured it was Brain calling back to say she would bring my backpack to school the next day. I ran into Mom and Carl's room and answered the phone.

It was Dad.

The call went like this:

"Hello?"

"This is the Federal Correctional Institution, South Florida. Is this Oliver Jones, Louisa Jones, Carl Wyatt, or Diane Wyatt?"

"This is Oliver."

"Please hold for Daniel Jones."

Click.

"Hello?"

"Hi, Dad."

"Hi, Spaghetti-O. Did your mom talk to you?"

"Yeah."

"I don't know what to say. I'm sorry."

"It's not your fault. This isn't fair at all."

"It's not fair, I know."

"This isn't right."

I didn't have anything else to say, really. I couldn't think past the fact that Dad hadn't done anything wrong.

Dad said a few more things about how disappointed he was and how he had been hoping this wouldn't happen, but honestly, I was only half listening.

I had taken the cordless receiver from Mom and Carl's

room into my room, and while Dad was talking, I was sitting on my bottom bunk, looking at my laundry hamper in the corner of the room.

One time I had to clean my room before Mom would let me go to Brain's house, and I was in a real hurry, so I just stuffed everything into the hamper. Clean clothes, dirty clothes, stuffed animals, even some old food wrappers. It was amazing how much stuff I could push down in that hamper without it overflowing.

Any feelings that came up while Dad was talking, I just stuffed them down into myself like my insides were a hamper. It worked amazingly well. Even when it sounded like Dad was crying, I didn't get upset. In fact, I didn't feel a thing.

WHAT'S NEXT

Mom said Louisa and I could stay home from school the next day if we wanted to, but we both said we wanted to go. Louisa didn't want to risk a single point on her grades, and I was hoping Brain and I could start planning how to help Dad.

But we didn't have a chance to discuss it until after school, when we were at my house to do our homework. Brain was on my bottom bunk with her math book and tablet, and I was on the floor trying to find the list of questions our teacher, Mrs. Thumbly, had given us for a social studies assignment.

"Maybe we can tell the judge that my dad didn't do anything wrong," I suggested.

"I don't know," Brain said. "If the judge didn't believe your dad, I don't think he would believe a kid."

"Maybe we can write a letter pretending to be Walker

Stewart and say he was the one who did everything wrong, not Dad," I offered instead, pulling a crumpled paper from my backpack that had something—grape jelly?—on it.

"Mmm-hmm," Brain said.

Mmm-hmm meant she was now totally focused on her math homework and had no idea what I'd just said. Brain loves schoolwork, and it's like she goes into a trance when she's solving math problems. There was no way I was going to snap her out of it, so I grabbed my social studies paper and Brain's phone and climbed up onto the top bunk to call Granny Janet.

Granny Janet, Carl's mom, is my step-grandma, and she's the second-meanest grown-up I know. She has long fingernails like painted eagle talons, and she says whatever she wants, even cuss words.

Granny Janet picked up after one ring. "What do you want?" she said.

"Hi, Granny Janet, it's Oliver," I began.

"I know who it is," she said. "What, you don't think I have caller ID? What can I do for you?"

"Oh, um . . ." I hesitated. "I am doing a report for school . . . on someone special in my family. And I picked you, because you are very special to me, Granny Janet." That wasn't true. First of all, we were supposed to pick an older relative, but Granny Janet wouldn't like it if I called her old. Second of all, I picked Granny Janet because she was the easiest person to get on the phone. Both Grandma Olivia and Grandma Darlene had passed away. My mom's dad, Grandpa Bo, lived in Texas and worked too late for me to call him on school nights, and my grandpa on my dad's side was . . . Well, no one knew where he was. My dad never talked about him, my mom said not to ask about it, and Louisa thought Dad had never even met him.

Anyway, that's why I called Granny Janet.

"It's supposed to help us better understand ourselves," I told her.

"This is what you're learning about in school? To call people in your own family? And the tuition at that cuss-word place is how much?"

"Um, we also learn to do presentations on something we are passionate about," I said.

Granny Janet snorted. "I should write a letter to that headmaster to tell him what I think of this school he's running. Teaching you to make phone calls and understand yourself. You can't put 'I understand myself' on a résumé, now can you, Oliver?"

"Um, probably not," I mumbled. I didn't know what a résumé was, but I didn't really want to know, either. "I just . . . I have five questions. I'm supposed to ask you about your past, present, and future."

There was silence on the other end.

"Granny Janet?"

I heard her sigh loudly. "This is a ridiculous assignment, but fine. Go ahead and ask your questions."

The first question I had come up with was about Granny Janet's childhood. "Did you grow up poor?" I asked. Granny Janet is rich, and I've noticed that most adults who are rich can't wait to tell you about how they grew up poor.

"Heck no, Oliver, my father owned a newspaper and three gas stations. We weren't poor. Next question."

I wrote *three gas stations, always rich* on my paper underneath the first question. Then I asked two questions about Granny Janet's life as a grown-up, and one question about stuff she likes to do now. The last question was about the future: "What are you looking forward to next in life?"

"Well, I'll have you know that less than three weeks from now I am receiving a major award in front of all my friends. It's at a dinner gala. I donated the most money to a charitable foundation."

Charity stuff, I wrote on my paper.

"What's the name of the foundation?" I asked.

"I can't remember," Granny Janet said. "Kids Something. They raise money to help kids, or people, or whatever. It's the foundation of that movie actor, Tony Skullwrecker. He has some sort of local connection."

"You mean *Tito the Bonecrusher*?!" I dropped my pencil.

"Yes, that's him."

"Can I go to the dinner?" I asked in the same breath.

"For Pete's sake, Oliver, it's three hundred dollars a plate, and they only sell them by the pair."

"Six hundred dollars just for two PLATES?" Rich people spend money on the strangest things. I had been trying to understand them ever since my mom first started bringing me to her housekeeping jobs, and every time I think I've figured them out, they do something else that boggles the mind. "How much does the *food* cost?" I wrote *$600—2 plates* in my notes.

Granny Janet sighed so loudly into the phone I had to pull it away from my ear.

"*Plates* means *tickets*, Oliver," she said slowly, like she was talking to a turtle. "It's two tickets for six hundred dollars."

I crossed out *plates* and wrote *tickets*.

"How's your father?" Granny Janet asked me.

"He's fine," I said. "I don't really like to talk about it."

"I don't blame you," Granny Janet said. "I wouldn't want to, either. And if anyone tries to get into your business, just tell them to shove it."

"Okay," I said. "Well, anyway, thanks for the interview, Granny. You were a big help."

"I sure was," she agreed, and hung up.

That was just like Granny Janet. She was getting to meet Tito the Bonecrusher, and she didn't even know who he was. Whereas I had been obsessed with Tito for as long as we had been watching wrestling with Dad, which was probably when I was about five days old. We had seen literally every Tito video together, from his lucha libre days at Arena México to his third, and final, UWE Championship. Dad said my first words were "Lucha! Lucha! Lucha!" But Mom says that's not true.

"Granny Janet is going to a fancy dinner with Tito!" I exclaimed to Brain. "Can you imagine? And she doesn't even know who he is." Rich-people stuff is almost always wasted on rich people, if you ask me.

"Hmm," Brain said, standing up from the bottom bunk and walking over to my desk with her tablet. "What's the name of the event?"

"Um, Kids Something," I told her. "My granny couldn't remember. Probably has to do with Tito's foundation." Granny Janet had said it was for helping kids, and Tito's charity, the Number One Fan Foundation, is all about helping kids.

Since we didn't know the name of the fancy dinner, Brain googled *Tito Bonecrusher, Number One Fan, Haselton, Virginia*. The first hit that came up was Tito's Wikipedia page, talking about the anonymous kid whose fan letter

28

had led Tito to start the Number One Fan Foundation. And the fact that Tito's former manager and movie sidekick, The Germ, is from Haselton. The Germ is the most famous person to come from Haselton, other than a writer named F. T. Robards, who writes long, serious books for grown-ups, and some lady who won big on *Wheel of Fortune*.

Brain kept scrolling till she found the link for the Number One Fan Foundation Gala: May 11 at the Empire Hotel.

The event web page said that the purpose of the gala was to raise money for the Number One Fan Foundation. Then it said: "The Number One Fan Foundation proudly welcomes both hometown hero Gerald 'The Germ' Casper and the #1 action star in America, Tito the Bonecrusher!" There were two boring pictures of Tito and The Germ; they were dressed in suits and smiling wide. Other than the fact that Tito was wearing the mask he always wears, they looked like two regular business guys. I prefer the action shots where they look extremely dangerous.

"Tito is coming here to raise money for the Number One Fan Foundation?" I asked. "How did we not *know* about this? Aren't your parents going?" I would have thought Brain's mom and dad would be all over this. They love fancy, expensive things.

Brain shook her head and pointed to something on the left side of the screen. "No way. The gala is being sponsored by Fluff Cream and Designer Mart."

Brain's dad, Mr. Gregory, owns a company called Apparel Warehouse, and Designer Mart is their biggest rival in town. Brain and her mom aren't allowed anywhere near Designer Mart or anything that has anything to do with Designer Mart. When I first met Mr. Gregory, he lectured me for twenty minutes on how the owner of Designer Mart is a swindler and a crook. And that was when I was six years old.

"Well, I guess I better write my report about Granny Janet," I said.

But Brain wasn't listening. She had started writing frantically on a piece of notebook paper.

This was typical Brain. If she needed to get some idea out of her head, she stopped everything and scribbled her thoughts until they were all on paper. After a few minutes, Brain shoved the paper in front of my face. There were words, numbers, arrows, dollar signs, and a bunch of exclamation points.

"What the heck is that?" I asked her.

"That," Brain said, "is how we are going to help your dad."

A BIG BELIEVER IN
SECOND CHANCES

On her scribbled-up paper, Brain had made a three-step plan to get my dad out of jail and back to Virginia in time for Louisa's graduation.

First, we would earn six hundred dollars and buy two tickets to the Number One Fan Foundation Gala.

Second, we would go to the gala, meet Tito the Bonecrusher, and ask him one question: *How do you break someone out of a federal prison?*

"Tito will know the answer," Brain said. "He said so on *Hollywood Tonight*."

That was true. In every movie he's done, Tito has had to get someone out of a bad situation: out of a laboratory, out of a space dungeon, out of a Wild West lockup . . . The list keeps growing. And in an interview about a year before, Tito had said that after all the research he'd done for his movies, he could rescue anyone from a bad situation. "I take my research very seriously," he'd told the host of *Hollywood Tonight*. "I interview security teams, study building schematics, and talk to experts." He said there was always at least one way, and usually two or three ways, to help someone escape from a secure facility if you really wanted to. "But I would never break the law in real life!" Tito assured the *Hollywood Tonight* host.

"Hmm," I said.

"Tito will know the answer!" Brain repeated, sounding confident.

"But Tito gets those people out illegally," I said, "not by talking to judges or lawyers or anything."

"Exactly," Brain said. "By any means necessary."

Which led to the third and last step of her plan: I would go to Florida and, using Tito's plan, rescue Dad so that he could keep his promise to Louisa.

"Tito's solutions are usually just a couple of steps, really," Brain said. "Bribe the right person, prop open the right door . . . you know how it works."

"But if it were that easy in real life, wouldn't people do it all the time?" I wondered.

"Not everyone has access to Tito the Bonecrusher," she pointed out. "But we will. And he *will* help us."

She was right. Helping people in bad situations was what the Number One Fan Foundation was all about. Tito had promised in front of an arena full of people to help kids who needed help. He promised. I was there, and I heard him.

I felt a buzzing of energy, and not in the bad, itchy-in-my-bones way that I'd felt after finding out that Dad had to go to prison in Florida. A good buzzing of energy, like when something important is missing and you look for it everywhere, and then you find it just in time. I had been waiting months for people to help my dad—the lawyers, my mom, even Walker Stewart—but no one had. Now the people who were going to help him were Brain and me. And Tito.

Brain and I got right to work on figuring out how to make the money for the tickets, and we knew we would have to use some of the signature moves we had recently developed from our extensive knowledge of Tito the Bonecrusher. The five signature moves are:

#1 Project confidence: Act like you know what you are talking about, even if you don't. Act like you are sure you will get what you want, even if you aren't. Tito does this all the time in his movies.

#2 Be extra friendly: If you treat the other person like you are their very best friend in the whole wide world, they are more likely to do what you want. You might even do them a little favor so they think you're really generous. This is how Tito's sidekick, The Germ, gets information from people.

#3 Take what you need without anyone noticing: I know it sounds like stealing, but "Sometimes you have to do what's wrong to do what's right." That's what it says on the poster for *Time Crusher 2: Out of Time*, which is my fifth-favorite Tito the Bone-crusher movie.

#4 Know a secret about the other person and threaten to tell it: You can get people to do all sorts of things if you've got a juicy secret about them. The Germ is AMAZING at this. He also did it all the time as Tito's manager when Tito was a professional wrestler.

#5 Make a deal with the person: If signature moves #1 through #4 don't work, you may have to trade something the other person wants for something you want. Tito did this in *Steel Cage 2: Back in the*

Cage, when (spoiler alert) he traded his scientist boss's secret science formulas so that his mother would be released from the laboratory where she was being held captive.

So far, we had used the signature moves only for minor schemes, like to get Brain's parents to let us stay up late or to get kids at school to switch partners so we could work together on a group project. But they worked for Tito the Bonecrusher. And they were the only signature moves we had.

To get money for the gala tickets, we came up with a harmless scam involving signature moves #1 and #2. It also involved signature move #3 and my stepdad, Carl.

Like his mom, Carl is really rich, but he hardly spends any money, which doesn't make any sense. He drives a beat-up Honda and wears jeans and T-shirts. He buys the jeans at the same wholesale place where we get our toilet paper and trash bags, and his T-shirts have sayings on them that don't make any sense, like I FOUGHT THE LAWN AND THE LAWN WON. If I was rich like Carl, I would spend my money on things that actually make sense, like my own limousine and lifetime tickets to UWE events. And on rescuing people from bad places.

The only thing Carl really loves to spend money on is

dorky computer gadgets like his fancy photo printer. It's supposed to be for his job, but he mostly uses it to print pictures of famous people and write goofy fake messages from the famous people to my mom. For example, he once printed a photo of this famous chef, Julia Child, and he wrote, "To Diane from Julia: Keep making that great mushroom casserole. It's your husband's favorite!" My mom thought it was completely hilarious and put it on the refrigerator with the other goofy pictures.

That gave Brain and me the idea to take some of the jokey photos and turn them into cash. We borrowed a couple of the pictures from the refrigerator (signature move #3) to use as examples. Then at recess on Wednesday, we told our classmates that thanks to my amazing stepdad, Carl, they too could have the autograph of any famous person for the bargain price of only five dollars.

We projected confidence (signature move #1) and acted extra friendly (signature move #2), and the next thing we knew, a bunch of kids were placing orders. Some kids wanted pictures with messages to themselves, like "Congrats on scoring a basket, Bobby! From NBA All-Star Stephen Curry." Others got photos for their friends, with notes like "Marco, I'm in your corner. Never quit trying! From Tito the Bonecrusher."

I sold six of Tito's pictures. I used the same picture for

every autograph: It's a classic photo of Tito from his first movie, *Steel Cage*, which was filmed right after he quit professional wrestling. A few other UWE wrestlers had done action movies, but Tito was the first masked one. And even though most of Tito's face is covered by his mask, it's amazing how scary he can look just with his eyes and mouth. He's not smiling at all, so he looks extremely dangerous. It helps that his mask for *Steel Cage* was designed to look like he was scowling at you.

Brain and I were raking in the cash so fast that on the third day of selling autographs, we got sloppy. I should have been suspicious when Brain's and my former friend, Sharon Dunston, asked me for an autographed picture of Clara Barton. I did what I'd done for all the other phony autographs: I printed Clara Barton's picture from the internet, wrote "Good luck in the spelling bee, Sharon! Love, Clara Barton" with a permanent marker, and handed it to Sharon at recess.

"That'll be five dollars, please," I said, holding out my hand so she could put money in it. Brain unzipped the fancy purse her mom had given her, which we were using as a cash register.

"Ha!" Sharon smirked. She marched across the playground to the teacher on recess duty. Brain and I stood and watched while Sharon pointed at us, waved the photo, and gestured dramatically. The teacher then sent us to Headmaster Nurbin's office.

I learned a couple of interesting things in Headmaster Nurbin's office. Turns out that (1) Clara Barton was a famous nurse who actually passed away a long time ago, and (2) there's a rule that you can't run a private business on school grounds between 7:30 a.m. and 3:00 p.m. So our photo-selling days were over.

Headmaster Nurbin said he was disappointed in us and told us we had to give back the money we'd made by duping students with forgeries.

Brain had been quiet up to then, but at this she cleared her throat. "To be clear," she said, "we never actually told anyone they were real autographs. It's not our fault if kids thought they were authentic."

"Did you tell them they were fake?" Headmaster Nurbin asked.

"I didn't think we had to," Brain said. She lowered her eyes and shook her head slowly, the way my mom does when she's not *mad*, just *disappointed*. "I thought Haselton Academy students would have better critical thinking skills."

She looked back up at Headmaster Nurbin.

He didn't go for it.

"The money will be returned to your classmates," he said.

"If they return the photos, you mean," Brain added. "They shouldn't get to keep them for free."

"Fine, Brianna," Headmaster Nurbin said.

There was a knock on the door. Someone from the main office needed to talk to Headmaster Nurbin.

"Don't go anywhere," he told us, stepping out of his office.

Brain looked over at me. Before I could freak out about the money, she said, "We shouldn't worry about this one. I have another idea."

Before I could ask what it was, Headmaster Nurbin was back.

He gave us a little speech about how, since he's a "big believer in second chances," we wouldn't get punished other than having our parents notified. But if we landed back in his office again, there would be "more serious consequences for your behavior."

Then he said, "You may return to class, Brianna." Brain and I both stood up, but he stopped me. "I would like to speak to you for just another moment, Oliver," he said.

Brain gave me a little nod, and I sat back down as she left the office.

Headmaster Nurbin leaned forward and folded his hands on top of his desk like he was about to announce something very important. "Oliver," he said, "I am sorry that this is our first conversation since you arrived at Haselton Academy this year."

"Oh, um, that's okay," I replied.

"I had wanted to welcome you to our school," he continued, "and tell you that we at Haselton Academy are committed to ensuring that all students get the help they need."

"Okay," I said. This was the weirdest conversation. "Could I please go back to class? I don't want to miss out on any more learning," I said in my most polite voice. "And don't worry, I won't be back in your office," I promised. "I've learned my lesson." *Learned my lesson that Sharon and I still definitely aren't friends*, I wanted to say.

The headmaster wrote a note to my parents about what Brain and I had done, and he said I needed to return it with my mom's signature. "Her real signature," he added. "Not another forgery like those autographs."

"Yes, sir," I said, barely listening. Instead I was thinking about the fact that our autograph scheme had failed and we were exactly zero dollars on our way to the gala tickets. But we would never quit trying. And apparently Brain already had a next step for our plan.

I had decided to do some research for our plan, the way Tito probably would, when Dad called at 7:00 that night. Mom used up a bunch of the phone-call time talking to him about the plans for Louisa's and my visit, so when it was my turn, I dove right in.

"Hi, Oliver. What's new?"

"I need information. I've got some questions about getting in and out of the . . . place where you are."

"For when you visit?"

"Um, sure."

"Okay, I can do my best to explain it."

"Is there any way in and out other than through the front entrance?"

"There's a back door to the yard where we spend time outside, but I think that's it. And all the visitors come in through the front."

"How do they bring in things for you? Like deliveries?"

"I think they all come through the front entrance. Are you planning to send me something? You can just bring it when you visit. I'll have Uncle Victor email you the rules."

"That's okay. I was just wondering."

"Mom said she got a note from the headmaster about you taking money from kids?"

"No, that was a big misunderstanding."

"You know you are very lucky to go to that school, Oliver."

"No, I'm not. The kids are jerks, and they rat people out."

"I know kids can be jerks," Dad said, "but don't let them ruin your education. Not everyone has what you have."

"I know," I said. Dad has always been hyped up about school and how it's important for my future and all that, but now it was like it was the only thing he wanted to talk about.

"How are your grades? Do you have any major assignments coming up?"

My grades weren't that awesome, so I ignored the first question. "Um, nothing too big . . . I think we have a science test next week."

"You're great in science!" Dad said. "You'll have to let me know how it goes."

"Okay," I said.

"You may not know that I had to leave school," Dad added.

"I know," I told him. "After high school." Dad didn't get to go to college, so he's kind of obsessed with it, and he asks a million questions every time he's around a college kid.

"Yes, but before that," Dad said. "I was out of school for a while when I was eleven, when we were moving a lot."

Dad's mom, my grandma Olivia, had had some problems, so the two of them had moved around, staying with aunts and uncles and stuff, before they settled down with Uncle Victor's family.

"That's . . . Isn't it illegal for kids to be out of school?" I asked.

"Sure," he said, "but someone has to come looking for you before it becomes an issue."

"Oh," I said. I couldn't really imagine being out of school and no one thinking it was a big deal. One time Louisa skipped health class to finish a math project, and when the attendance office called our house, Mom's whole head turned red and almost popped right off.

"It was a complicated situation," Dad said. "Sometimes I wonder . . ." He kind of trailed off. "It doesn't matter. Things happen and you just keep going. But anyway, Spaghetti-O, do yourself a favor and stay out of trouble at school. Do your work and keep your grades up. That would be a big help to me."

Yeah, right. That wasn't a "big help." That was the kind of "help" you assigned to someone you didn't think could help at all. Like when I was little and my job at Dad's restaurants was to "help" count the spoons. And then Louisa told me that counting spoons wasn't a real job; it was just to keep me out of the adults' way.

Tito the Bonecrusher wouldn't stay out of the way.

"I gotta go," I told Dad. "I'll . . . Let me see if Louisa is here."

"Okay," Dad said quietly.

Louisa had refused to talk to Dad every time he'd called from jail.

I knocked on Louisa's door. "Are you here?" I asked.

"No," she said from the other side of the door.

"She says . . . she's not here," I told Dad. "I'm sorry."

"It's okay," Dad said quietly again.

We hung up.

After I got off the phone, I watched Tito's old lucha libre videos on the internet for an hour. It was awesome. If you ever want to know more about something like lucha libre, or you need to keep your feelings pushed down, I recommend watching videos on the internet.

SMASHFEST

Conversations with Dad had never been so serious before. Usually we would talk about wrestling, or Dad would repeat funny or ridiculous things his coworkers had said, or we would make plans for our next visit. I reminded myself that it would be like that again, after we rescued Dad from FCI South Florida.

After Mom and Dad got divorced, but before Dad moved to Florida to help Walker Stewart open the new steakhouses, Dad's apartment was just a couple of miles from Mom's. Louisa and I would go back and forth between them. At Haselton Academy, the kids I know with divorced parents have these tight schedules, like they go to their dad's at exactly 4:00 p.m. on Friday and return to their mom's at exactly 4:00 p.m. on Sunday.

For Louisa and me, it had never been like that. Since Dad worked at two different restaurants and Mom ran her own housecleaning business, their work schedules were all over the place. Sometimes we would be with Dad for days at a time, sometimes for just a few hours. Basically one parent would babysit us while the other one had to work. "Mom and Dad can't afford to hate each other," I remember Louisa reassuring me once, back before she was either ignoring me or mad at me all the time.

If we were with Dad on nights he wasn't working, we would watch wrestling. Sometimes it was UWE, and sometimes it was lucha libre, depending on the TV schedule. The lucha libre stuff we mostly watched online. By the time I was old enough to follow wrestling, Tito was already big in the UWE, but we would watch old matches from when he competed in Mexico. My dad's favorites were the matches in Mexico City at Arena México. Dad had been a lucha libre fan since he was a teenager, when some of the older guys at his first restaurant job introduced him to it and would invite him over to watch old tapes of matches and luchador movies. "It was like my substitute for watching sports with a father growing up," Dad told us once.

We were all big wrestling fans, but Louisa probably knew the most about it. She followed a bunch of UWE websites and could tell us what the rumors were about upcoming events, what was unscripted during matches, and why UWE would turn good wrestlers bad or bad wrestlers good. And she would get really annoyed if you used the wrong wrestling terms.

Even though Tito had started using American pro wrestling moves when he joined UWE, his wrestling style was still more like lucha libre, which meant wrestling against him was like getting your butt kicked by a super-strong acrobat. He flipped and leapt around the ring in ways that always surprised you. People say Tito quit wrestling because he couldn't handle the moves anymore and he couldn't risk losing his mask. But they're wrong. He has *never* been unmasked. And he never will be.

A few years ago, when he still lived in Virginia, Dad said he was taking a Saturday night off to take Louisa and me on an adventure, but he wouldn't tell us what it was. He said we could each bring a friend, but all of Louisa's friends were busy, so I invited Brain plus Sharon, who was still our friend at the time. We were all together at Brain's house while my mom was working. Brain spent the early part of the afternoon trying to figure out where we were going. "It's probably within a thirty-minute drive of here," she said, and she studied a map for the possibilities, cross-checking it with the local online listings of activities suitable for kids. Our list included Disney on Ice; a high school singing competition; something called Bible Mania at the Baptist church in the next town; and the usual kid-friendly activities like go-karts, roller-skating, and the movies. Brain puzzled over the list for a while, and then she turned to me.

"We're going roller-skating," she announced. Brain and I both looked at Sharon. She had worn her fanciest party dress, which was pale pink and covered in lace, in case the surprise was a royal wedding . . .

"What?" Sharon said. "I can roller-skate in this dress."

At 4:30, my dad picked us up in his van. Louisa was already with him. He drove us to Samburgers, a hamburger place run by this guy named Sam. We used to eat there all the time.

"Samburgers is our surprise?" I said, trying not to sound too disappointed.

Dad just grinned and ordered a big tray of burgers and fries. The five of us sat down, and Sharon put like twenty napkins all over her lacy dress. Dad pulled out an envelope.

"The surprise is somewhere else," he said, "and it's about an hour away, so we should eat first."

Brain gave a little yelp when he said an hour away.

He handed the envelope to Louisa. She peeked inside. "Yahoooooo!" she exclaimed.

"What is it?" I demanded.

She pulled out some tickets and handed one to each of us. They said:

UNITED WRESTLING ENTERTAINMENT PRESENTS: SMASHFEST

Brain and I stood up and danced around. "Wrest-a-ling! Wrest-a-ling!" Brain loved to watch wrestling with us at Dad's apartment, but none of us had ever been to an actual live match before. I noticed that the tickets were pretty expensive.

We wolfed down our burgers and fries and headed back to the van. During the whole ride to the arena where SmashFest was happening, we were basically bouncing in our seats. Louisa was going on and on about everything that was supposed to happen at SmashFest.

"There's a rumor that Tito the Bonecrusher is coming to this one," Louisa said.

"People say that every time," Dad said, kind of chuckling at Louisa. "They are still saying that every time there's a big match at Arena México, and he hasn't wrestled there in years."

"A lot of people are saying it this time," Louisa argued.

"Like, reliable sources. They say he's going to return to make some kind of big announcement."

The SmashFest excitement was in the air before we even got into the arena. People were selling stuff in the parking lot, and as we got closer to the door, we saw people walking around holding up signs saying they wanted to buy tickets or had tickets to sell.

We went inside and made our way to our seats. They were up kind of high, but that was good because we could really see everything. There was music thumping and intense images of wrestlers on screens.

Suddenly the arena got dark.

"The power's out!" Sharon shrieked.

"Shhh," Louisa said.

A loud voice boomed, "UWE fans! . . . Are you ready for SMASHFEST?!?"

A bunch of lights started flashing everywhere, the music started thumping louder than before, and then the show started.

It was awesome. It was just like watching it on TV, except you could feel the energy of thousands of other wrestling fans, right there cheering and booing with you. Even Sharon was getting into it. The only downside was that they had these firework things that *boomed* when different wrestlers entered, and every time it happened

Sharon would scream in my ear. She was way too jumpy for professional wrestling.

The way SmashFest works is that there are a couple of matches between wrestlers who are famous but not super famous, and then there is the SmashFest Showdown, which is between some of the biggest-name wrestlers in the UWE. The night we went to SmashFest with Dad, the Showdown featured a wrestler named Triple Threat, who was known for his three toughest moves and his catchy theme music, and this completely mean wrestler named Fists O'Blarney who wore shiny green pants and had a giant shamrock tattoo on his face.

When Triple Threat entered the arena to his theme music, everyone went wild, cheering and clapping and just yelling. When Fists O'Blarney came in, people booed loudly.

"It's rude to boo," Sharon said, shocked.

"It's okay here," Dad told her. "It's part of the show."

Despite all the cheers, things started looking bad for Triple Threat right away. Fists O'Blarney started slamming him around. He even jumped out of the ring, grabbed a chair from the announcers' table, and smacked Triple Threat with it. Triple Threat went down hard.

The announcers sounded worried. "This Showdown is not going well for Triple Threat," they said, even though it was obvious. "He's trying to get back up, but—"

Just then Fists O'Blarney slammed his opponent down again. The ref blew his whistle and made a motion to signal that the match was over.

I thought Fists would grab the mic and brag or something, which is what most wrestlers do when they win, but he wouldn't leave Triple Threat alone! He went over to him and kicked him! The boos got louder and louder. Louisa even said a cuss word.

The ref was shouting at Fists O'Blarney that he was in violation of UWE rules. Fists walked over to the ref and started arguing with him, then shook his head and walked back over toward Triple Threat.

Just then there was a commotion at the announcers' table. The announcers started hollering, "Someone is entering the ring! Someone is entering the ring!"

We could hear a wave of cheers and shouts building from the lower level of the arena and spreading all around.

Sharon started looking around all wild-eyed. "What is happening? Is it an emergency?"

"TITO!!!" Louisa screamed, pointing.

"It's Tito the Bonecrusher!" one announcer's voice boomed right after Louisa's. "The rumors are true!"

That's when we saw him. Tito was on the floor of the arena, walking toward the announcers' table near the ring.

Once he was really close to the table, an announcer

held out a microphone to Tito so that he could speak. Tito reached out a hand and took the microphone, but he didn't even look at the announcers. And instead of stopping to make an announcement, he kept walking. He walked right up to the ring and climbed in!

Triple Threat, who was still lying on the canvas, lifted his head. He looked shocked, from what we could tell on the jumbotron monitor showing close-ups of the ring. And Fists O'Blarney looked furious.

"That ref told you the match was over," Tito said to Fists. "And you're still kicking a man when he's down."

"So what?" Fists O'Blarney growled. "This isn't an action movie. There are no stunt doubles. You're not a real wrestler anymore, Tito, and you know it. You can't stop me."

"Yes I can," Tito said. He took a step toward Fists and pointed at the shamrock tattoo on his face. "You're gonna wish you had more four-leaf clovers," Tito warned him, "because your luck is about to run out."

"Oooooooh," Brain and I said at the same time.

"But you're going to have to wait, O'Blarney," Tito said to Fists. Then he turned, held the microphone to his mouth, and started to speak to the crowd. "I didn't just come here tonight to take care of this punk O'Blarney." His voice sounded serious. "I need to share something with all the Bonecrushers."

The crowd started cheering again.

"Are the Bonecrushers his family?" Sharon asked.

"It's his fans. He calls us Bonecrushers," I explained.

"I left UWE a year ago, after my third SmashFest championship," Tito said. "Since then, thanks to you Bonecrushers, I've had more blockbuster movies than any other wrestler in the history of UWE." Tito continued describing all the amazing success he'd had with his movies and merchandise and everything. "I hear from you Bonecrushers all the time, whether you come to see me at appearances, reach out online, or send letters."

"A little while ago I got this letter from a young Bonecrusher," he said, pulling a piece of paper out of his pocket and unfolding it with his free hand. "And I'm going to read it now."

He launched right in:

"Dear Tito,

I love to watch your movies. You are so exciting and you always tell people to never quit trying. Your movies make a lot of money. You always help people in the movies, so I was wondering if you help people in real life, too. For example, we don't have enough money to pay our rent, and we are going to

54

have to move out of our apartment and live with my cousins. They already don't have enough space. But lots of people have even more problems than that. Some kids don't have enough food or coats or other things. I was thinking maybe you could use some of your money to help them. I think this is a good idea.

From your number one fan."

Tito paused. "Then there's a name. A child's name. I'm not going to read his name on camera, but I do have something to say to my number one fan."

The arena was totally silent. The jumbotron screen showed close-ups of a bunch of people in the audience, and some of them were wiping tears from their faces.

"What's 'rent'?" Sharon asked, clutching the lace on her party dress. Louisa and I shushed her.

Then the camera zoomed in on Tito, who looked directly into it.

"Number One Fan," he said, as if that little kid was there in the arena with him, "I'm so proud to have a fan like you—someone who wants to help people, unlike O'Blarney here."

"Oh, boo-hoo," Fists fake-cried, grabbing the letter

from Tito. "It's just some letter from a little kid. Little kids *love* Tito the Bonecrusher."

"That kid needs help," Tito said. He snatched the letter back from Fists. "Maybe you should help someone for once in your life."

"Ha!" Fists laughed. We could even see him roll his eyes at Tito, because we were watching everything on the jumbotron. "I'm not some weak little do-gooder."

"Well, you're about to be," Tito said, "because I'm challenging you right here and now, Fists O'Blarney, to a lucha de apuesta."

Dad, Louisa, and I gasped.

"Oh YEAH," Brain said.

"What's that? What's *that*!?!" Sharon wanted to know.

She didn't have to worry. Tito always super-explains all the lucha libre stuff because most Americans don't know anything about it.

"A match with a wager," Tito continued. "If I win—and I *will* win—you must promise to give one hundred thousand dollars to help this kid."

We couldn't believe it! A hundred thousand dollars was a lot of money.

"And what happens when you lose?" Fists O'Blarney sneered.

"Oh, O'Blarney." Tito chuckled and shook his head.

"I am certain that I won't lose to you. But if I do, I will give the same amount of money to you," Tito said.

"I don't need your money," Fists growled. "I want something bigger. And I know you won't take this bet, because you know you won't win. *I* will win, and when I *do* . . ." He paused dramatically.

"What?!" Sharon shrieked, and I swear the whole arena glared at us.

"When I do win," Fists continued, "then I get to unmask you."

"Ohmygah," Louisa said under her breath.

"And the whole world," Fists went on, "gets to see the face of a sellout and a coward."

I glanced at Louisa. She looked like she was ready to run down to the ring and fight Fists O'Blarney herself.

"Deal," Tito said. He reached out his hand so that he and Fists could shake on it.

But Fists didn't let go after the handshake. Instead, he yanked Tito toward him, and SLAMMED his knee into Tito's stomach. Tito fell to the mat.

"Boooooo!" the crowd called.

"THAT'S SO DISRESPECTFUL!" Sharon screamed.

The ref began to count. "One, t—"

Tito was on his feet before the ref could say two. He ran toward the ropes, jumped up, launched himself off the top rope, and whipped his leg around to kick Fists in the head. Fists toppled sideways into the ropes, but then bounced right back to his feet.

It was definitely one of the best wrestling matches I had ever seen, and not just because I was seeing it live—it was also extremely intense. All five of us were on the verge of a total freakout when Fists had Tito pinned to the mat and we thought it was the end. Sharon had to bury her face in her hands, Louisa was hollering "Get up!" and I think my dad was muttering a prayer under his breath. Absolutely no one in that arena wanted to see Tito unmasked, other than Fists O'Blarney.

The ref started counting. "One . . . two . . ."

Tito jerked his shoulder up off the mat just in time.

"YEEEEESSSSSS!!" Louisa screamed.

Within seconds, Tito had gotten out of the hold, flipped Fists around so that his shamrock tattoo was pressed against the mat, and pinned him. The ref started counting. Fists was trying to get up, but he couldn't. The ref got to three. The arena went wild.

As soon as Tito released his hold, Fists staggered to his feet, stepped out of the ring, and stomped off.

Tito was on one knee and breathing hard after that match, but he stood up and signaled for someone to pass him a microphone. "O'Blarney will give the money to help my number one fan," Tito said. "I'll make sure he does. But it's not enough. My number one fan asked me to help other people in need. I hear you, my young fan, and today, with some of the money I have earned thanks to the support of my Bonecrusher family, I am going to start a foundation for children. And I'm going to start it with ten . . . million . . . dollars."

I thought the crowd had gone wild before, but it was nothing compared to what happened when Tito said he was giving ten million dollars to help kids.

The arena had to be on the verge of exploding from all the excitement happening inside it. Dad, Louisa, Brain, and I stood up and whooped. The crowd started chanting, "Ti-to! Ti-to! Ti-to!" Even Sharon joined in.

Everyone except Dad, who was driving, of course, fell fast asleep on the way home from SmashFest. Dad dropped off Brain and Sharon, and then he took Louisa and me back to his apartment, where we slept hard after all that cheering.

The next afternoon when Dad dropped us off at Mom's, the two of them had another surprise for us. It was a family meeting. That was when Dad told us he was going to be moving to Florida. At least for a couple of years, he said, to help a man named Walker Stewart get some new steakhouses started.

I was sad.

But Louisa was angry. "You knew? You knew all last night and you didn't tell us?" Her face was red and scowling.

"I didn't want to ruin your fun at SmashFest," Dad said.

"You lied to us," she fumed. After that, she was mad at Dad for weeks. And she wouldn't watch wrestling with us again.

I thought about that SmashFest pretty much all the time. Not just about the wrestling, but about Tito's number one fan. I wondered who the kid was, what he did with Fists O'Blarney's money, and whether all his problems got solved. I also wondered whether Tito could solve problems that money couldn't fix.

BRAIN'S BIRTHDAY

Brain's new gala-ticket-moneymaking idea involved signature move #3: **Take what you need without anyone noticing**. In this case, the *anyone* was Brain's parents. Brain was turning eleven that Sunday, and she always gets a bunch of checks on her birthday. And after Headmaster Nurbin took the autograph money that was rightfully ours, Brain suggested that we sneak-use her birthday money to buy the gala tickets. Her parents usually deposited her birthday checks in her savings account, so it wasn't like she ever saw the money anyway. Brain said that this year, we would cash the checks ourselves and just tell her parents that to be financially responsible, we took the checks to the bank. "Technically we are taking them to the bank. We're just not depositing them," Brain told me.

It was hard to predict how much the total amount

would be. There was a chance that we could get really close to the six hundred dollars we needed to buy the tickets. (When I first started going to Brain's birthday parties, I could not BELIEVE how much money she got from her relatives.) It was also possible, however, that the total could be much lower. Some years it's low because instead of all money, she'll get these "heirloom" gifts from her grandparents. Stuff like very expensive silverware with curlicues etched on the handles, or super-breakable china plates. I guess Brain's grandparents want her to throw a dinner party or something. We were crossing our fingers extra tight this year that she was going to rake in the cash instead of fancy spoons.

Brain and I have celebrated her birthday together since we were six, when my mom used to clean her house. Even though Mom ran the housecleaning business and had a couple of assistants, she did a lot of the cleaning herself, especially for her longtime clients like the Gregorys. She sold the business to her assistants when she married Carl because she didn't want to work in the same neighborhood where she was living, and now she teaches classes on how to run your own business.

Anyway, when I started celebrating Brain's birthdays with her, it was way before my mom married Carl and we moved to his ritzy neighborhood. Back then I saw Brain only on Saturdays when my mom was taking care of her house, and then I would stay and play at the Gregorys' while my mom and her team cleaned a few other houses nearby. But then, on Brain's sixth birthday, she insisted that her mom invite me to her party.

Brain's mom used to invite half of Haselton to Brain's birthday parties, which had themes like Princess Tea Party or Royal Teddy Bears—basically anything that gave Brain's mom an excuse to wear a tiara. Brain got so tired of greeting her mom's friends and thanking everyone for coming that on her ninth birthday, she rebelled and insisted on wearing a lucha libre mask. She told everyone she was La Diabólica, the champion luchadora, and she may have even threatened to use La Diabólica's finishing move, the powerbomb, on a couple of party guests. So that was the end of the princess parties. The next year her mom let her invite just Sharon and me for a sleepover, and this year, it was only me.

In honor of Brain turning eleven, I had gotten her a special-edition DVD set of the most important Tito movies ever made: *Steel Cage* and *Steel Cage 2*. I had seen *Steel Cage 2* three more times since Dad, Louisa, and I watched it in the movie theater, and somehow it got more amazing every time. The three-disc set I'd gotten for Brain included "not only both *Steel Cage* and *Steel Cage 2: Back in the Cage*, but also never-before-seen footage and a commentary track by Tito the Bonecrusher himself." Those were the exact words from the commercial for the DVD set, and Brain and I had seen the commercial so many times we had pretty much memorized it.

After dinner, we sat in the living room so that Brain could open her birthday presents. Before she could get to my gift, we had to suffer through some of the gifts from her parents. She got another manicure set, some stationery with unicorns on it, and three dresses.

I have this great-aunt in Chicago I haven't seen since I was four, and when she sends me gifts, there's usually a note that says something like "The lady at the store said these are very popular with boys your age!" That's how it was with Brain's parents. Based on the gifts they bought her, you'd think she was someone they hadn't seen in years.

"The lady at the store said these are very popular with girls your age," Brain's mom said as Brain opened a package that contained a set of jewelry shaped like cupcakes.

"Thank you." Brain's voice was flat but polite. She extracted the cupcake bracelet from the plastic wrap and put it on her wrist.

"Oh, how adorable!" Brain's mom cooed. "Oh, Warren, just look at Brianna. WARREN!"

"Mmmm, lovely, Jessica," Brain's dad said, not looking up from his phone.

Once we got through the random presents from Brain's parents, it was time for the checks.

"A hundred dollars from Grandmother and Poppy . . ." Brain barely glanced at the card before reporting the amount on the check. "Yes! Two hundred dollars from Nana and Roger . . . five dollars from Aunt Hazel." Brain kept going until every envelope was opened. "Four hundred thirty dollars total," she announced as soon as she'd opened the final envelope. Like I said, Brain is practically a genius.

We were still short on cash. Brain and I exchanged looks.

"Can you excuse us for a moment?" Brain asked her parents.

She didn't wait for an answer. She ran up the stairs to her room, and I followed her.

"We're close," she said as I shut the door behind me. "We need less than two hundred dollars."

"Brain," I said, "I know how we can get it." I paused. "Signature move number five." I had an idea for how we could **make a deal with the person**—or people, in this case.

Brain narrowed her eyes. "Go on," she said carefully.

I must've looked kind of shifty, because she seemed to know I was about to say something she wasn't going to love.

"We can do the commercial," I said.

Brain wrinkled her nose like she was smelling garbage.

For years, Mrs. Gregory had been trying to get Brain to act in a commercial for Mr. Gregory's company, Apparel Warehouse. *You have such a pretty face when you're not squinting behind a book,* she'd complain. Brain had always refused. Her mom also tried *It would mean so much to your father,* but we all knew Brain's dad couldn't care less who was in the commercials as long as they convinced people to shop at Apparel Warehouse.

Brain sighed deeply several times, then stared up at the ceiling like she was hoping a better idea would fall through the roof or something. It didn't.

She looked back at me and nodded. "Signature move number five," she said.

We hustled back down the stairs, where Mrs. Gregory was trying on Brain's new cupcake jewelry and Mr. Gregory was typing on his phone.

"Mom and Dad?" Brain said, trying to get their attention. Only Mrs. Gregory looked at her. "I've decided that I'll do a commercial for Apparel Warehouse."

Brain's mom almost fainted.

"Just one," Brain added firmly.

Brain's mom clapped her hands together, and the little cupcakes made a jingling sound. "Oh, Warren, isn't this wonderful? . . . WARREN!"

Brain's dad glanced up from his phone.

"Brianna is going to do a commercial for Apparel Warehouse!" Brain's mom sang *Apparel Warehouse* like *she* was the one in the commercial.

Before Mr. Gregory could go back to his phone, Brain laid out three conditions: (1) The commercial would be filmed as soon as possible; (2) I had to be in it, too; and (3) we each had to get paid.

"We'll pay you whatever you want," her mom said.

"Now hang on a second, Jessica—" Brain's dad began.

"Thirty thousand dollars," Brain said immediately. She knew from the movies that you should ask for more than what you need.

"How about fifteen dollars," said Brain's dad, who also seemed to know the rules for making a deal. He and Brain went back and forth until they eventually settled on one hundred dollars for each of us.

A hundred dollars each would put us over the top.

I called my mom to ask about the commercial. You'd have thought she would be excited for her only son to become a television star, but she wasn't. "You don't need any more distractions," she said. "I'm already concerned about your grades. And the note from the headmaster—"

"That was a one-time thing. I didn't do anything wrong. My grades will be *amazing*. Please, Mom. It'll make me really happy. Don't you want me to be happy right now?" Nothing wrong with laying on a little guilt.

Mom sighed into the phone. "Okay, but no more visits to the headmaster's office. And no bad grades."

"Deal," I said. "'Night, Mom!" I hung up before she could make me promise anything else.

At last, it was time for Brain to open my present. Whenever Brain and I give each other gifts, the person receiving it tries to guess what is in the package before opening it. To throw Brain off, I had taped the DVD case to the bottom of a much bigger box so she wouldn't automatically know it was a movie.

Brain lifted the package and shook it. "Is it something to wear?" she asked.

"Nope!" I said.

"Is it a book?"

"Nope!"

"Hmm . . . Is it spy equipment?"

"Nope!"

"Hmm . . . Is it sports-related?"

I considered this. "Sort of," I said. "It has to do with . . . Yes, sort of sports-related, in that—"

"Oh for the love of money, just open it, Brianna," Brain's dad interrupted. "I have a conference call with Singapore in ten minutes."

Brain ripped into the package.

"Woo-hoo!" Brain exclaimed. She jumped up, and the wrapping paper went flying.

"What is it, Brianna?" Brain's mom said. Now she was typing on her phone. Probably telling half of Haselton about Brain's commercial.

"*Steel Cage*! Both movies!" Brain was already ripping the plastic wrap from the DVD case. "We *have* to watch these tonight," she declared.

We dashed to her rec room, where she had her own entertainment system.

Mrs. Gregory wandered in a few minutes later. "Don't you want your cake, Brianna?"

"We can have it in here," Brain said, her eyes not leaving the TV screen as she scrolled through the DVD menu. I turned to give Mrs. Gregory a thumbs-up, but she was already looking at her phone again.

We started with the original *Steel Cage*, where Tito the Bonecrusher first plays Bruce Paxton, the former professional wrestler, and he has to break his brother out of a criminal gang's headquarters. Brain and I watched it like twenty times when we were figuring out the signature moves, but the new DVD had the director's cut, with four minutes of never-before-seen footage, so it was like seeing it again for the first time.

We were about three-quarters of the way through the movie when the clock hit 8:30 and, as I expected, Brain's dad made us go to bed so that he and Mrs. Gregory could have some peace and quiet. Brain and I lay low in her room, waiting patiently for her parents to go to bed at ten o'clock. Technically, Brain waited patiently and I fell asleep, but Brain woke me up when the coast was clear. Then we snuck back to the rec room and watched the rest of *Steel Cage* and all of *Steel Cage 2: Back in the Cage*, which is a lot like the original *Steel Cage*, except that Tito has to rescue his mom instead of his brother.

Every Tito the Bonecrusher movie is kind of the same, which is what makes them so awesome. You always know what to expect. Tito plays a former pro wrestler who now has a job that requires him to be super strong, like a bodyguard or security guard or something. Then some evil villain takes someone important to Tito, and he has to rescue them through some elaborate plan. The plan usually involves sneaking into a secure facility, and also wrestling.

The other thing in every movie is that Tito never, ever takes off his mask. Some people say he has never been seen without his mask in real life. There are a couple of controversial photos that people say are of Tito, but no one can prove it. Brain says they are obviously photoshopped, and she's practically a genius, so I believe her.

Some people say it's silly that Tito's character wears a mask in every movie, but my dad always said that it was a sign of strength and pride. Tito never tried to hide that he was a luchador and not some regular old American wrestler. Sometimes Dad would get all fired up talking about wrestling and masks. He said it didn't matter what anyone said about Tito's mask.

Some people also say it isn't true that every movie features The Germ because The Germ didn't have a speaking role in *Steel Cage 2: Back in the Cage*, but you still see his face, so I think it counts. Brain does, too. Our opinions are the same on most Tito controversies.

Anyway, after the second movie, we started on the bonus features even though I could barely keep my eyes open. At some point I must have fallen asleep on the couch, because I woke up to Brain smacking me on the shoulder.

"Get up, Spaghetti-O! It's morning! We have to go upstairs before my parents wake up!"

We raced upstairs to Brain's room and pretended to be asleep when her mom came in to wake us up five minutes later.

It was awesome. But in all the excitement, I had

forgotten that we had a science test that day. Which was going to make it really hard to keep my promises to Mom and Dad about my grades. Which was why later that day I found myself standing in front of my teacher's desk, trying to convince her that I hadn't cheated.

THE SCIENCE TEST

The rest of the class was at recess. It was just me, Sharon Dunston, and Mrs. Thumbly, who kept staring at me. Her stare reminded me of Tito's movie *Time Crusher*, which features these evil robots who shoot laser beams out of their eyes, and the only person who can stop the robots is Lance Knightfox, the former pro wrestler turned masked security guard played by Tito the Bonecrusher. It's only my fourth-favorite Tito movie, but it's still amazing.

I had never cheated on a test before, so I wasn't sure how to react. I tried not to blink. And I tried not to look down and to the left, which according to Lance Knightfox is a classic sign that you're lying. That's how, in *Time Crusher 2: Out of Time*, he figured out Senator Corruptron couldn't be trusted.

"I didn't cheat?" I told Mrs. Thumbly. Shoot. It

probably wasn't very convincing to say it like a question. I tried again. "I didn't cheat."

Mrs. Thumbly maintained her suspicious glare while Sharon wept noisily beside me.

"Really," I insisted, ignoring Lance Knightfox's other rule of looking completely innocent, which is to keep your mouth shut and don't say too much. "I studied my head off. I studied the cytoplasms and the mito-, um, the . . . all that other great stuff you taught us about plant and animal cells. Fascinating stuff, Mrs. Thumbly."

Mrs. Thumbly frowned. "I certainly do think it is fascinating, Oliver, considering that cells are the building blocks of life."

"I completely agree?" I said.

"I wish I could believe you passed this test on your own, Oliver," Mrs. Thumbly said, not looking like she wanted to believe me at all, "but you and Sharon chose the exact same answers, even for the questions you got wrong."

I hadn't planned to cheat, but when I got the test and didn't know any of the answers on the first page, I started thinking about my dad and the stuff he'd said about school. And I really wished I'd done some studying. My eyes blurred a little bit, and when they refocused, I realized I was looking at Sharon's test paper. I could see all of her answers. And I automatically started copying them. I guess you could say I used Brain's and my #3 signature move: **Take what you need without anyone noticing**. It wasn't that I really wanted Sharon's test answers, I just wanted . . . I don't know what I wanted, exactly.

For most of the test, it had been easy to avoid detection because Sharon practically had her nose pressed against the test paper, she was reading it so carefully. But on the next-to-last question, Sharon looked up right when I was checking out her answer sheet.

We locked eyes. Sharon clenched her jaw, got up from her seat, and marched to Mrs. Thumbly's desk. Mrs. Thumbly walked over to me, took my test paper, and walked back to her desk without saying a word.

So that's why I was standing next to the teacher's desk during recess, saying I didn't cheat.

Sharon was crying and carrying on like she'd been accused of murder. "I swear to God I'm innocent, Mrs. Thumbly! I would never allow anyone to copy off me! Especially not Oliver. Even if I would ever allow someone to copy from me—and I never, ever would—Oliver would be the very last person I would ever let copy my work! I swear! You have to believe me!" she sobbed.

It's one thing to proclaim your innocence, but Sharon didn't have to get so personal.

It wasn't like I'd really wanted to copy from Sharon, either. Sharon Dunston is a jerk, a snitch, and a two-faced priss. But I was panicking, and it just happened.

"How do you know that Sharon didn't copy from *me*?" I asked Mrs. Thumbly.

"Be serious, Oliver!" Sharon cried. I was being kind of serious. I usually get good grades, just not when I have more important things to do, like help my dad when nobody else will.

Mrs. Thumbly glanced at the clock. We had to be approaching her lunchtime, which gave me an idea. "I'll retake the test right now if you want," I said, bluffing. "Right here in front of you." I figured there was no way Mrs. Thumbly would sacrifice her lunchtime to sit and watch me take the test again.

Mrs. Thumbly and Sharon were both silent.

I rambled on. "I bet I can get an even higher score than I did before. And if I don't, you can go ahead and say I cheated." I tried to project confidence like Tito does. He's really good at bluffing.

"Okay. That seems fair," Mrs. Thumbly said.

Shoot. That never happens in Tito's movies.

Sharon grabbed a tissue to wipe her eyes, mouthed "You're lying" at me, and scurried off to lunch. I sat down at my desk, and Mrs. Thumbly gave me a new test paper and a multiple-choice answer sheet. I reread the first question:

Janie is a scientist who has prepared slides of plant and animal cells. Look at the pictures below of Janie's microscope slides. Which of the slides is LEAST likely to be an asparagus cell?

I wanted to march up to Mrs. Thumbly's desk and ask her when in my life I would ever need to identify an asparagus cell, but I knew she would give me a lecture on the building blocks of life. This was hopeless. I hadn't known any of the answers the first time, so it wasn't like I was going to know any of them this time.

I tried to picture Sharon's answer sheet in my head. I thought the first answer was C, maybe? Or B. Then I remembered that when I'd finished copying Sharon's answers, I'd thought the answer sheet looked kind of like the Big Dipper.

I went through and filled out the answer sheet to look kind of like the Big Dipper. Then I handed the test back to Mrs. Thumbly. She made me wait while she graded it. When she finished, the paper was covered with so many red dots that it looked like my answer sheet had the chicken pox.

"This is an F, Oliver," Mrs. Thumbly said.

I looked down.

"Wait—" she started, and I looked up. "Actually, it's an F minus. I forgot we gave those, it's been so long since a student got one."

Then she sent me to Headmaster Nurbin's office.

HEADMASTER NURBIN'S OFFICE 2: BACK IN THE OFFICE

"Hello again, Oliver," Headmaster Nurbin said when he finally saw me. I had been sitting on the leather bench in front of his office for a long time. At my old school, the bench in front of the principal's office was metal with red peeling paint, and kids would scratch things into the paint like THIS SCHOOL IS TERRIBLE, which wasn't true but was probably what you're thinking when you're on the principal's bench about to get in trouble. But Headmaster Nurbin's leather bench looked brand-new and really expensive.

I handed Mrs. Thumbly's note to the headmaster when I walked into his office. While he read it, I settled into one of the cushy, deep brown leather chairs and waited for his "I'm a big believer in third chances" speech. Or maybe he would ask *why* I cheated. I'd gotten a really high score on the test you have to take to get into Haselton Academy, so he must have wondered what was going on with me.

"Well, Oliver," Headmaster Nurbin began. He wrinkled his nose and set down Mrs. Thumbly's note like it was a dirty tissue. "I suppose your previous school did not prepare you academically for the rigors of Haselton Academy."

I started to say that the work here was actually kind of easy compared to what my teachers had given me the previous year, after they'd decided I needed to be "challenged," but Headmaster Nurbin kept talking.

"No matter how difficult the work may be," he said, "there is never an excuse for cheating. You need to take some time to think about your behavior. So you will complete a Saturday Service Reflection."

This sounded familiar from when I'd skimmed the Haselton Academy Code of Conduct at the beginning of the school year, but I didn't remember any specifics.

"You will report to school on Saturday from nine a.m. until one p.m. You will work with our high school service coordinator, Mr. Pollson, to beautify our school grounds."

"Oh. Like detention," I said.

Headmaster Nurbin cleared his throat. "We don't give detention," he said calmly. "Detention is a punishment. Saturday Service Reflection is an opportunity for you to reflect on your behavior."

"Okay," I said, even though it sounded exactly like detention to me. "Let me check my agenda."

I opened my backpack and took out a pencil and the fancy leather agenda book that had been issued to me when I started at Haselton Academy. They must have a deal with some leather company, because everything is leather around here. I flipped to the month of May and scanned for an available Saturday. May 18 had FLORIDA in big letters. May 11 had GALA on it. And this coming Saturday, May 4, was the filming for the commercial.

Brain and I had to have that commercial money. It was our last chance to earn cash before the gala.

"Hmm," I mused. "I'm busy the next three weekends, but I can do the last Saturday in May." I started penciling DETENTION THING in the box for May 25.

I looked up to see Headmaster Nurbin watching me. His expression was less like the we-are-all-friends-here headmaster smile that had surprised me on my first visit to his office, and more like the principal-who-is-fed-up-with-you face that I'd seen once or twice at my old school.

"It's not about doing it when it's convenient for you, Oliver," Headmaster Nurbin said. "Reflection time must happen as soon as possible, to discourage you from engaging in inappropriate behaviors like cheating. Do you know who you're really hurting when you cheat?"

"No one?" I offered. Cheating doesn't really HURT anyone, not like punching someone, or sending somebody to prison when they didn't do anything wrong.

"You're really hurting yourself," Headmaster Nurbin said. "Because you're cheating yourself. Out of knowledge."

I tried to raise my hand to protest, but my arm was kind of stuck to the stupid leather of the chair. My eyes started to itch.

"But this weekend I have to—"

"Your reflection time is this Saturday, May 4." Headmaster Nurbin's voice was stern, like my mom's when she's really, really done arguing.

"Yes, sir," I said.

While Headmaster Nurbin typed up a letter about my Saturday Service Reflection, I sank down in the ugly leather chair and thought about how everything would be ruined when Mom got this letter. Now Brain and I definitely wouldn't have enough money for our tickets. Which meant I would never know how Tito the Bonecrusher would help me rescue my dad. Which meant I wouldn't be able to rescue him. Which meant nobody would.

Headmaster Nurbin handed me the letter, a tissue, and a pass back to class. "Stop in the restroom on your way back," he advised me in a much nicer voice, "and splash some water on your face so no one can see you've been crying."

"I'm not crying," I told him.

I left his office and headed straight to the boys' bathroom.

☆ 8 ☆

THE WRATH OF BLANKY

By the time I got back to class, there were only about five minutes left before dismissal. Then it was time for another nearly silent ride with our bus driver, Mrs. Blanky.

Mrs. Blanky is the meanest grown-up I know. She's meaner than Fists O'Blarney and John Rancid combined.

She has been driving a bus for about two hundred years, and even though she's totally horrible, the parents love her. They think she's this sweet old lady. At the end of my second week at Haselton Academy, my mom made me give Mrs. Blanky a box of homemade cookies, a gift certificate to Starbucks, and a handwritten card. Here's what I had to write:

Dear Mrs. Blanky,

Thank you for welcoming me onto bus 179!
You are the world's greatest bus driver. I
appreciate that you safely drive me to and
from school each day.

Sincerely,
Oliver Jones

Here's what I wanted to write:

Dear Mrs. Blanky,

You are DEFINITELY NOT the world's
greatest bus driver. Every night I get down
on my knees and pray that you win the
lottery so you will retire and I no longer
have to deal with your outrageous bus
rules. You are truly disturbed.

Sincerely,
Spaghetti-O

Mrs. Blanky has a long list of her super-strict rules
posted at the front of the bus. Most of them are about how

you have to sit. If you break the rules, you will catch the Wrath of Blanky.

Fortunately, Brain taught me all about the Wrath of Blanky while we waited for the bus on my first few days. She told me the story of how one year a girl named Penny broke the rule that you can't put your window down while the bus is moving, so Mrs. Blanky drove the bus through a car wash so that Penny and all the kids sitting around her got soaked. One version of the story is that it was the middle of winter, so the kids were frozen into human icicles, but Brain said she's not convinced of that part.

Brain also told me the story of a boy named Wesley. Wesley broke Mrs. Blanky's rules over and over, and one day Mrs. Blanky had had enough, so Mrs. Blanky let him out at the side of the road and he had to walk all the way home. Another version of the story is that Mrs. Blanky waited until all the other riders got off the bus, and then she drove Wesley all the way to the West Virginia state line and let him out there, but Brain isn't convinced of that one, either.

Brain also told the Mrs. Blanky stories to this kindergartner, Joey Muffaletta. It wasn't pretty. When Brain told the story of Penny, Joey started to cry, and he cried straight through to the end of the story of West Virginia Wesley.

But you better believe that little Joey Muffaletta has followed every single one of Mrs. Blanky's rules, and he hasn't caught the Wrath of Blanky. He can thank Brain for that.

Here are some of Mrs. Blanky's rules:

- You must sit with your spine pressed up against the back of the bus seat or you will catch the Wrath of Blanky.
- You must keep your knees together, and under *no* circumstances can you put a knee or foot into the aisle or you will catch the Wrath of Blanky.
- If you want to talk, forget it. You can't even talk to your seatmate. Since you have to keep your spine pressed up against the back of the seat, you can't really turn your head to look at your seatmate, but eventually you kind of get used to whispering while you're staring straight ahead. If you lean all the way forward or if your voice goes above a whisper, you will catch the . . . Well, you know.

Louisa says I'm a gullible sucker for believing the legends about the Wrath of Blanky. Just because I believed in the tooth fairy until I was in the fourth grade, Louisa says I'll believe anything. But she doesn't have to ride bus

179, so she doesn't understand that you can never be too careful.

And anyway, sometimes you have to let yourself believe stuff even if deep down you're afraid it's impossible. If that makes me gullible, then I'm okay with it.

Brain and I are assigned to seat twelve on bus 179, and a kid named Popcorn Robards sits between us. Brain, Popcorn, and I are the only kids who have to sit three to a seat. That's because Brain and I are on the small side for fifth grade, but we're going to hit our growth spurts any day now, and Popcorn is the smallest of all. Popcorn will probably hit his growth spurt when he's twenty-five, if he hits it at all. That's why he goes by Popcorn—because he looks like a popcorn shrimp.

Popcorn will never catch the Wrath of Blanky because he never says a word. I mean, he says "Hi" to us when he gets on the bus and "See ya" when we get off the bus, but for the rest of the ride he's silent. When he told us his nickname at the beginning of the year, I thought we might become friends, because it's not every day that you meet another person who's nicknamed for a food. But Popcorn prefers to keep to himself, so he sits silently while Brain and I whisper back and forth. (I think the quiet helps our minds work better; Brain and I worked out most of the signature moves on the bus.) I think Popcorn is especially terrified of Mrs. Blanky because he's so small and she could crush him like Tito crushed the mastermind behind the robot technology in *Time Crusher 2: Out of Time*.

Earlier this year, Mrs. Blanky took a corner too fast, ran into a mailbox, and came screeching to a halt. Everyone on the bus screamed, and Sharon Dunston fainted. We all had to get out of the bus and stand around in some guy's yard while the police came and wrote some kind of report. The guy wasn't too happy about having a busload full of schoolkids trampling his grass, and he was extra cranky because he had just bought a new mailbox.

Even through that whole wild afternoon, Popcorn didn't open his mouth one time.

So other than the fact that we were both new at Haselton Academy, I didn't know very much about Popcorn. It was Brain who told me that Popcorn's dad was this famous writer who writes long, serious books for grown-ups and is always on those boring public television interview shows. One of his books won some kind of prize that I had never heard of.

Anyway, on the way home that day, I had to tell Brain the news. "I got detention—I mean, Saturday Service Reflection—from Nurbin," I whispered, staring straight ahead. "So I can't shoot the commercial."

There was a long pause. As usual, Popcorn didn't say a word, and the whole bus was nearly silent.

"There is no way I'm doing this without you," Brain whispered back. "I didn't want to do it in the first place. Besides, we won't have enough money without your hundred bucks."

"Obviously," I hissed. I was being a little bit mean, even though it wasn't Brain's fault.

Brain was too focused to notice. "We have to think," she whispered. "What would Tito do?"

"I have no idea." I really didn't. "Tito hasn't gotten detention in any of his movies."

"I bet Tito would use a decoy," Brain replied, "like in *Time Crusher 2*."

That was probably right. In *Time Crusher 2: Out of Time*, Tito's character, Lance Knightfox, gets some guy who kind of looks like him—tall and dark-skinned, with super-beefy muscles—to wear his clothes and a spare mask and take some of Senator Corruptron's henchmen on a wild-goose chase. Meanwhile, Lance Knightfox breaks into the space dungeon and rescues his uncle, who also happens to be the president of Earth.

The bus pulled up to the corner of Culverton and Main.

"Mr. Jiggly Fluff!" I heard little Joey Muffaletta say excitedly and much too loudly from the seat in front of us.

"SEAT ELEVEN," Mrs. Blanky's voice boomed from the front of the bus. "NO TALKING. YOU ARE IN VIOLATION OF RULE SEVEN. THIS IS YOUR FIRST AND LAST WARNING."

"Mr. Jiggly Fluff," little Joey whispered mournfully.

Then I heard quiet sniffles. If Mrs. Blanky yells at a kindergartner or first grader, the kid always cries. Guaranteed.

I took the risk of turning my head to look out the window. Sure enough, there was Mr. Jiggly Fluff, or rather, an employee of the Fluff Cream Dairy Dessert Shop dressed in the giant inflatable Mr. Jiggly Fluff costume. Mr. Jiggly Fluff was standing on the corner and holding a sign that said ONE BUCK WEDNESDAYS . . . ALL SMALL FLUFFS JUST $1! The sign had a picture of a cone with a swirl of soft-serve Fluff Cream on the top. Fluff Cream doesn't look or taste any different from regular soft-serve ice cream, but little kids go wild for Fluff Cream because they all love Mr. Jiggly Fluff. They think he's their best friend or something.

I like Fluff Cream fine, but I definitely didn't think Mr. Jiggly Fluff was anybody to get all excited about. Especially since Mr. Jiggly Fluff stands on the corner of Culverton and Main at least three days a week.

Thanks to little Joey's outburst, Mrs. Blanky was sure to have her eye on our corner of the bus, so it wasn't worth the risk to continue talking to Brain. I would have to wait until we got to her house to figure out how to never quit trying.

The bus rolled along for another block or two until I heard a little *whoosh*, like someone letting air out of a balloon or a tire, or like when the wind blows through the trees in a cheesy Disney cartoon movie that you watched only because you were bored, not because you were obsessed with it or anything.

"What was that?" I whispered to Brain.

Brain ignored me. I knew she didn't want to risk getting in trouble. Brain had priors.

I heard the air-whooshing sound again, but this time it sounded like words, as though the wind was saying *I'll do it*. I shook my head. I figured I was hallucinating from not having enough sleep before the science test.

About thirty seconds later, the bus slammed to a stop. The door screeched open and Mrs. Blanky said flatly, as she does every day, "Seats eleven, twelve, and thirteen: Your stop. Get out."

My seatmates and I shuffled off the bus. I was last. My shoes had barely touched the pavement before the door shut, Mrs. Blanky floored the gas pedal, and the bus was gone.

I turned to Brain. "We better get going," I said.

"See ya, Popcorn," Brain said, giving Popcorn and the kids from seats eleven and thirteen a half wave as she and I started walking.

"I'll do it," Popcorn said.

THE DECOY

Brain and I stopped walking and stared at Popcorn. He stared back.

I blinked. "Do what?" I asked.

"I'll take your place in Saturday Service Reflection," Popcorn said, "but I need to make a deal with you. Signature move number five."

I was stunned. Since Popcorn never talked, it hadn't occurred to me that he would have been listening to Brain and me figuring out the signature moves. I'd almost been thinking of him as a statue, like a less creepy version of the old-fashioned children made of stone that Granny Janet has scattered around her fancy garden.

"You know the signature MOVES?" I asked Popcorn.

Popcorn's answer didn't make any sense. "My dad says a writer has two tasks: observing the world, and writing the essential truths of what has been observed."

"Um, okay," I said.

Brain looked sharply at the kids from seat thirteen, including Sharon Dunston, who were still hanging around the bus stop. "Beat it," she commanded. They all hustled away, except for Sharon, who crossed her arms and huffed.

"Let's take this conversation inside, boys," Brain muttered to Popcorn and me. "The walls have ears, you know." She raised her eyebrows like we were supposed to know what that meant, and Popcorn nodded.

We hustled up the sidewalk to Brain's front door. There was no time to waste, except the time we needed to spend gathering snacks. We walked past Brain's mom and into the kitchen. Mrs. Gregory was so wrapped up in her favorite reality show, *Fancy Wives of Male Models*, that she didn't seem to notice that we'd brought an extra kid home.

The Gregorys' pantry shelves are LINED with junk food that I never get at home. Brain grabbed two bags of potato chips, and I took a box of this amazing cereal called KidzNuggets that glows in the dark. We headed farther down the hall to Brain's rec room. When my mom was the Gregorys' housekeeper, it used to drive her bonkers that there were crumbs wedged everywhere in the rec room furniture.

We settled in on the L-shaped couch with our snacks. Brain handed a bag of potato chips to Popcorn.

"So what's the deal, Popcorn?" Brain said with a mouth full of chips.

"I, um, I could be Oliver's decoy," Popcorn said. He was looking down at the potato chip bag as he crinkled it in his hands. "I don't look like him, but I think it would work out."

"We're listening," Brain said carefully.

Popcorn laid out a plan: Since he and I were both in our first year at Haselton Academy, the teacher in charge of Saturday Service Reflection didn't know either of us. So Popcorn could show up at detention and claim to be Oliver Jones. Meanwhile, I would be at the commercial shoot pretending to love my corduroy pants or whatever I was wearing from Apparel Warehouse.

I almost hollered *Sure!* This was a great plan. No detention! But I glanced at Brain, who gave her head a slight back-and-forth shake, and I realized that we needed to hear the other end of the deal.

"What do you want from us?" I asked.

"I want to meet Tito," Popcorn said.

Well, that was a problem. We would have only two tickets to the gala. Obviously I needed mine the most because I had to find out from Tito how to rescue my dad, but Brain deserved the other one because it was almost all her money that we were going to be spending on the tickets.

I turned to Brain, who was expressionless.

"I need to consult with Oliver," she said to Popcorn.

He nodded, and then he hopped up and scooted toward the door. "I'll be in the hall," he said.

As soon as he was out the door, I looked at Brain. "This is weird, right?" I said. "That he would offer to do this? How well do you know this kid?"

"Not much better than you do," Brain said. Popcorn had moved to the neighborhood just before I did, and in case I didn't already mention it, the kid really kept to himself. "But I think he'll hold up his end of the deal."

"It's not a good deal," I argued.

"Eh, I think we go for it," Brain said. "I mean, better for one of us to go than neither of us."

Brain hadn't specified who would be the "one of us" to go, her or me. "So when you said 'one of us,' did you—"

"Obviously it should be you, Spaghetti-O." Brain rolled her eyes. "It's your dad we are trying to save."

I wondered what was in it for Brain now. We were using all her money, and she wasn't even going to get to go. But I didn't want to ask. I didn't want to poke any holes in the plan, or I might cause Brain to change her mind.

"YOU CAN COME BACK NOW, POPCORN," I called.

Popcorn scooted into the room.

"You can have my ticket to the Number One Fan Foundation Gala," Brain offered casually, leaning back against the couch as if it were no big sacrifice, "if you get through the detention without getting caught."

"Why do you want to meet Tito so much?" I asked Popcorn.

"I just do," Popcorn said. "Why do you want to meet Tito so much?"

"I just do," I told him.

That evening, the phone rang at exactly 7:00—Dad's usual call time—and I ran to Mom and Carl's room. But when I picked up the receiver, I heard someone else already on the line: Louisa.

I should have hung up, but I didn't. As far as I knew,

this was the first time Louisa had spoken to Dad since he'd had to go to jail.

"This is Louisa Jones."

"This is the Federal Correctional Institution, South Florida. Please hold for Daniel Jones."

Click.

"Hello?"

"Hi."

Dad's voice immediately sounded shaky. "Oh, Louisa. Hi. I'm so glad it's you."

What was that supposed to mean? I replayed it in my head. *I'm so glad it's you.* I was the one who had been willing to talk to Dad since the first night we found out about his sentence, whereas Louisa was being kind of dramatic about it, really. And I was the ONLY PERSON who was trying to help him. *I'm so glad it's you.* He had never said that to me.

But Dad would feel differently after I was the one who rescued him. I made myself refocus on the plan and the signature moves. I imagined every step, from earning the rest of the money to buying the gala tickets to actually meeting Tito and figuring out how to rescue Dad. I started to feel better again.

"Yeah, I just . . . ," Louisa responded. "You know what, I actually can't do this. I'll get Oliver."

Thinking about the plan had helped me push the bad feelings back down. I had been starting to feel better for a second. Or at least, I was feeling nothing, which was better than feeling bad. So when Louisa hollered for me to pick up the phone and talk to Dad, I pretended I didn't hear her.

THE APPAREL WAREHOUSE COMMERCIAL

Unlike my stepdad, Carl, Brain's dad really knows how to act like a rich person. He has a shiny luxury car with leather seats and satellite radio, and he orders people around on the phone like rich businessmen in the movies do. He is the owner of all eight Apparel Warehouse stores across the mid-Atlantic, so if you've ever done back-to-school clothes shopping at Apparel Warehouse, you have made Warren Gregory a little bit richer.

Riding in Mr. Gregory's car was pretty much the only glamorous thing that happened on May 4, the day of our commercial shoot. We had to shoot the commercial before the store opened that morning, so it was still dark outside when I walked over to Brain's house. Inside, Mrs. Gregory was already making Brain and her dad so bonkers that I was afraid Brain was going to cancel the whole thing.

"If there are any speaking parts, make sure they consider Brianna. Brianna would be the logical choice since she is your daughter, Warren." Mrs. Gregory went on like this to Mr. Gregory for another billion minutes before turning to Brain. "Brianna, remember to be personable and smile. You can be so charming when you want to be. Wear whatever clothes they ask you to wear. And if they put you in dresses, don't tell them you're allergic to the fabric." She turned back to Mr. Gregory. "Warren, she is not allergic to any fabrics. Be sure she doesn't tell whoever's doing wardrobe that she's allergic to the fabric. Who's doing wardrobe? Is it—"

"Stop freaking out, Mom!" Brain interrupted. Then she turned to me. "Let's go, Oliver." She ran out the door, ready to get the commercial over with before her mom could make her promise to star in any more of them.

During the luxury car ride to Apparel Warehouse, Mr. Gregory explained what the commercial was going to be. The idea was basically a montage of happy people shopping at Apparel Warehouse with a cheery song playing in the background. But they only wanted to show a few people at a time.

"We want it to look popular but not too crowded," Brain's dad explained. "We don't want people to think they will have to wait in long lines."

Brain and I were going to be paired up with adults who could be our parents in the shopping scenes. We didn't know who those adults would be, since we were a last-minute addition to the commercial, but Mr. Gregory said he was sure it could all be worked out.

There were already a couple of people setting up when we got to Apparel Warehouse. Mr. Gregory pointed out the director of the commercial and introduced us to the wardrobe lady, Elyse.

"No Mrs. Gregory today?" Elyse asked.

Mr. Gregory shook his head, and Elyse looked pretty relieved.

Once we had our clothes figured out, Elyse said it might be a while before we got called over to film our part of the commercial, so Brain and I sat down in a corner of Apparel Warehouse under a table of white shirts that all looked the same and a sign that said MEN'S SHIRTS 3 FOR $30, WOMEN'S SHIRTS 2 FOR $60!

"If we are going to be waiting a while, we might as well do our homework," Brain said, unzipping her backpack.

"Fine," I sighed. I had thought that starring in a commercial would be a little more glamorous than it actually was. With all the waiting around, I could understand how Tito got so much reading and exercising done when he was making movies.

Lately, "doing our homework" had kind of turned into Brain doing the homework and me copying it. I couldn't really concentrate on anything other than our plan to rescue my dad. I started writing lists of questions for Tito and drawing diagrams of what the inside of FCI South Florida might look like. When I had my chance to talk to Tito, I wanted to be prepared.

I had finished copying the math homework and was now copying Brain's personal essay, which was about last year's spelling bee.

"She might know you copied this one," Brain said, "since you didn't even go to our school last year."

"Whatever," I said. I had zero interest in telling my personal business to Mrs. Thumbly. I'm not the type to go blabbing to anyone who will listen.

I finished copying Brain's essay and moved on to the social studies homework. "And the Native Americans sold Manhattan to the Dutch because kgjasklgkgflg," I wrote. I tried to write as messily as possible so Mrs. Thumbly wouldn't notice that I copied. She never read the homework all the way to the end, anyway. She just checked to make sure there were plenty of words. She'd given me a B on my report about Granny Janet, and the only thing she said was that the interview with my "aunt" should have been longer.

As I was scribbling, Brain tapped me on the arm and

then pointed to where all the commercial action was happening. There was some kind of commotion. Brain's dad was talking to Elyse, the director, and a few other people. We crept up behind a rack of skirts and listened.

"Why weren't these casting decisions made last week?" the director snapped at Mr. Gregory.

"Henry, we only need them in one shot. I'll never hear the end of it from Jessica," Mr. Gregory complained.

"I can pair Brianna with Helen"—the director gestured at a blond lady fixing her makeup who looked like she could be related to Brain—"but we don't have anyone who looks related to that boy."

"That's fine, whatever," Mr. Gregory said, "as long as Brianna appears on camera."

"No way!" Brain stepped out from behind the skirt rack and crossed her arms. "You said both Oliver and I would be in the commercial. And that we would both get paid. A hundred dollars each."

"But we don't have an adult who—" Brain's dad started to reply.

"We don't need ADULTS," Brain argued. "Just shoot some footage of Oliver and me looking happy in the store. People will assume our parents are offscreen."

Brain knows a lot of film terminology like *offscreen* and *footage* because we've listened to the directors' commentary tracks on so many Tito DVDs. She also knows I don't like to get upset in front of people, and not getting the commercial money would've made me pretty upset. That's Brain for you. A real friend sometimes fights back for you before you even know you need it.

"And besides," Brain continued, "it's just a montage. People don't care if it makes sense. If they see happy people and hear happy music, they'll want to shop here."

The adults all stared at Brain.

"She has a point," Elyse said.

"Fine," the director sighed.

He set up a shot in which Brain and I were trying on hats and smiling into a mirror, like we were having the best day of our entire lives. We had to do it about ten times, but then we were done.

"Okay, that's a wrap. Go get in the car," Mr. Gregory said.

"Where's our money?" Brain asked.

Brain's dad pulled out his checkbook and wrote us each a check for a hundred dollars. "There you go," he rumbled.

Brain and I whooped and cheered and high-fived. We had done it! We had six hundred dollars!

"And no talking or loud music on the way home," Mr. Gregory said, rubbing his temples. "I have a headache."

☆ 11 ☆

A SURPRISE FOR YOU

As soon as we got to Brain's house, we dashed upstairs to her room to add our checks to Brain's birthday money. "The rest of them are on my—" Brain stopped, looking confused. "The checks *were* on my desk."

Brain's desk was bare except for her tablet, her keyboard, and a couple of notebooks. She looked under the notebooks. Nothing.

"Maybe you stuck them in a drawer?" I offered.

"I know where I put things," Brain said, sounding panicky but also speaking the truth.

Brain is very organized. She began looking through the drawers anyway, and I started helping her.

We heard the garage door open, and a few minutes later Mrs. Gregory's voice called up the stairs. "Brianna! Come down here, darling! I have a surprise for you!"

Brain turned to me, panic in her eyes. "I have a very bad feeling about this."

We thundered down the stairs and into the Gregorys' living room, which looked like another holiday gift-buying commercial. There were shopping bags everywhere. In the middle of them was Mrs. Gregory, smiling so big you could see her back teeth, which didn't have veneers on them.

"Brianna!" she gushed, sounding out of breath. "To celebrate the beginning of your modeling and acting career, I booked you a session with . . . Javier Flambeau!"

"Who?" Brain and I said at the same time.

"Brianna! You know Javier! He was at one of my cocktail parties last year! He's the best headshot photographer in the mid-Atlantic. He's very expensive, but he's the best." Mrs. Gregory took a breath and then continued talking. Her eyes were shining brighter than her extra-white teeth. "And I know we always deposit your birthday money in your savings account, which is a very boring tradition, so your father agreed that this year you could have . . . a NEW WARDROBE!"

When Mrs. Gregory said the words *new wardrobe*, she made this jazzy motion with her hands, and then she waited for Brain to react.

I don't know what Brain's reaction was. My heart was thumping in my ears and my vision was getting kind of blurry, so I couldn't look at her.

Mrs. Gregory started digging through the bags and pulling out clothes. "These clothes will photograph better than those baggy ones you've been wearing, Brianna. Aren't they fun?"

She was waving two things at Brain that I think were shirts. One looked like a zebra pelt, and the other one had a bunch of ruffles on the sleeves.

"How much of my birthday money did you spend?" Brain said in a whisper barely louder than the one she uses on the school bus.

Mrs. Gregory laughed. "Brianna! Your birthday money was just the starting point! But don't tell your father that. Here, let me show you everything—"

"You spent all my birthday money?" Brain cried.

"Yes, darling, but you're always saying you forget you even have it, since we deposit it every year—"

"It was mine!"

Brain's not the type to get all blubbery, which is one of the reasons we are best friends, so it was strange to see her start to lose it—so strange that I hadn't really thought about what she and her mom were saying.

Now Mrs. Gregory looked confused and maybe angry. "But I spent it on *you*," she said. "I thought you'd be grateful."

Brain turned around and bolted up the stairs.

Mrs. Gregory looked at me. Her eyes were all watery

and her makeup was getting messed up. I'm not good with people having emotions in front of me. Plus, my heart was racing from the news that Mrs. Gregory spent our four hundred bucks on a zebra pelt and some ruffles.

"Um," I said. "I guess I . . . um."

"*I* guess you should go home now," Mrs. Gregory told me. "Your mother—who I'm sure you always treat with respect, unlike how my Brianna treats me—will want to hear all about your day. I know you love your mother."

"Oh, I'm pretty sure Brain loves you," I said. "She just wants you to like her, even though she doesn't really care about tiaras or makeup or . . ." I looked around. "Or zebra clothes."

I gave a little wave goodbye to Brain's mom but didn't say anything else. I can make a quick exit when I need to.

I ran home, thinking *Gone, gone, gone* with every step. If Brain's birthday money was gone, our gala-ticket money was gone, which meant our opportunity to meet Tito was gone. Which meant any teeny-tiny chance of finding a way to help my dad was gone. *Gone, gone, gone.*

I tried calling Brain about twenty times on Saturday and Sunday, but she didn't answer until late Sunday afternoon.

"I haven't thought of anything yet," she said in a rush before I could say a word, "but I'm working on it. I asked my mom to return the clothes, believe me, but she wouldn't let me use the money for the gala tickets. We'll figure it out, though, Oliver. Never quit trying."

"Should I call Popcorn and tell him?" I asked.

"Let's keep thinking," she said. "And if we can't think of anything by tomorrow after school, we'll tell him then."

12

IT'S MORE COMPLICATED
THAN THAT

I told myself I would stay up all night to think of a new plan to earn the money, but I couldn't do it. I closed my eyes for a second, just to rest them, and the next thing I knew Mom was shaking me awake and telling me to get ready for school.

I missed the bus, so she had to drive me. When I got to my classroom, Brain was standing by Mrs. Thumbly's desk, so we didn't get to talk. I started the day feeling pretty stressed out.

There was less than a week left before the gala. It had been just two weeks since we'd learned Dad had to go to prison, and it had been barely six months since we'd found out Dad was in legal trouble. I should say, it had been barely six months since *Louisa and I* found out. Our parents (including Carl) knew sooner, but no one bothered to tell us.

The first hint had come back in November. I guess I should have known something serious was going on when Louisa actually started a conversation with me. I was in my room, lying on my bed and reading the comic-book version of *Coyote Willis*, when she came in.

"Are you . . . What are you looking for?" I asked. "I didn't take anything of yours."

Louisa rolled her eyes at me, which was pretty much her favorite hobby. "I'm not trying to ACCUSE you of anything," she said. "I just wanted to see what you know about what's going on with Mom and Carl."

"Like right now? They're at a meeting."

"No, I'm talking about how they've been acting so strange."

I hadn't noticed anything other than Mom and Carl being boring grown-ups. I told Louisa that. She looked at me like I was the most ignorant person on the planet.

"You're kidding, right?" she said. "I keep catching them talking to each other all serious, like, *whispering* to each other. Then when they notice me, they start smiling and being all cheery."

I did remember that, the day before, Mom had shut her laptop super fast as soon as I walked into the living room.

"Maybe they are planning some kind of big surprise for us," I suggested.

Louisa frowned. "I don't know. I don't think it's anything good."

"Maybe Grandpa Bo is sick or something," I said. Grandpa Bo, Mom's dad, lives in Texas, so Mom and Carl would have to make travel plans for her to go see him if he was really sick.

"Maybe." Louisa looked unsure. Then her face tightened again so she would be ready to roll her eyes at me on a moment's notice. "But, listen, don't be stupid and say something to Mom or Carl about this," she warned me.

"Okay," I said.

It was just the very next night when Mom told Louisa and me that she needed to talk to us in the living room. It was a "please sit down" conversation. Louisa said it was the same weirdly calm voice Mom had used before, when she and Dad told us they were splitting up. Basically, if your parents ever tell you in a super-nice voice to please sit down, you're about to get bad news.

It took me a while to figure out what Mom was saying. She went into this whole long story about Dad and Walker Stewart, and how sometimes people treat each other terribly and she kept using the words *issue* and *situation*.

"Wait, so Dad got fired?" I asked. "He has to get a new job?"

"No, the situation is more complicated than that," Mom said. "It's possible . . . The issue is that we don't—"

"Oh my God, Oliver," Louisa said. "He didn't get fired—he got in trouble with the government. The other restaurant guys got caught lying about money. Obviously, they are like total criminals."

"How was that obvious?" I asked. "How was *I* supposed to know?"

"Oh my God," Louisa said again. "It's not about *you*."

Mom interrupted us to say a bunch of stuff about how we should be kind to each other at this stressful time and how family was most important and how we had to lean on each other.

"It's more of a *hassle* for your father than anything else," Mom said. "Just a headache that's going to take up a lot of his time. He had to get a lawyer, and he's going to work with Uncle Victor until everything is resolved. But I thought you should know. And I will try to answer any questions you have."

"Is Dad guilty?" Louisa asked.

"Of course he's not guilty!" I said. "You're the one who said the other restaurant guys are criminals!" It was like Louisa wasn't even listening to herself.

"I didn't ask you," Louisa snapped.

"Your father was a loyal employee," Mom said. "He trusted Mr. Stewart, maybe too much. And now Walker is trying to blame your father for his own illegal decisions."

"Walker Stewart is a cuss word," Louisa said, "And Dad should have known it. Walker Stewart is a lying cuss word who can go cuss word in the cuss-word cuss word, until the devil cuss words his cuss word."

Carl coughed from the next room.

Mom made about three faces in a row. The first one was a watch-your-language face, the second one was a you're-not-wrong face, and the third one was . . . I don't know what it was. Like her face was frozen onscreen over a bad Wi-Fi connection, but in real life.

"Why are YOU telling us this instead of Dad?" Louisa asked Mom.

I don't know how she does it, but Louisa can say "YOU" and it's like she's punching you in the face.

Mom's face turned red, and her lower lip got all quivery. She grabbed a tissue from a box on the coffee table and wiped her eyes. She held the box out to me. I stared at it. She put it back on the coffee table.

"We thought it would be better for me to tell you in person instead of having Dad tell you over the phone. I know you probably want to talk to your father. You can call him now if you want."

I wanted to, even if Louisa didn't, and I picked up the phone right away. Dad sounded totally normal, almost cheery.

"Everything is going to be fine," he said. "It's just a pain because I have to do all this paperwork. Plus, I'm gonna need earplugs if I'm working with Victor all day."

Uncle Victor's voice has one volume level: loud.

When Dad told me everything was going to be fine, I could feel my whole body relax. That was what he always said when something got messed up. Like once when I was playing with a pen, and the ink exploded all over Dad's favorite blanket from Grandma Olivia, and Dad washed it out so I would stop crying my face off. Or another time when he left work early to drive me to the pumpkin-patch field trip in first grade because I had been in the school bathroom and missed the bus.

Obviously, I didn't know then that everything *wasn't* going to be fine. Neither did Dad. And he hadn't known it when we last saw him in Florida, either.

Anyway, that's what I was thinking about after I showed up late to school on Monday, and when Mrs. Thumbly called on me during social studies, I had no idea what the question was. I didn't even hear her until she'd said my name a couple of times. Some of the kids giggled.

"Quit laughing," Brain barked at them. She looked at Mrs. Thumbly. "The Hudson River," she said, which I guess was the answer to the question I hadn't heard.

Mrs. Thumbly nodded at Brain and then looked back at me. I waited for her to send me to Headmaster Nurbin again, but instead she just nodded at me, too, and then asked a question to another kid.

13

BUS RIDE 2: BACK ON THE BUS

Brain and I were going to wait until we were off the bus to tell Popcorn the bad news about the money, but after a whole day of keeping my thoughts to myself about our failed mission to save Dad, I was out of patience. When we got on the bus Popcorn smiled so big at us that I couldn't take it anymore.

"Brain's mom spent all our money," I whispered, pressing my spine against the back of the seat. "We can't get the tickets."

"Guess we're not gonna wait," I heard Brain mumble.

There was silence from Popcorn.

"I'm really sorry," I continued, whispering to Popcorn. "You did my Saturday Service Reflection for nothing."

It sounded like Popcorn was sniffling, but he still didn't say anything.

"We know how much you wanted to meet Tito," Brain whispered from the other side of Popcorn.

"I have to meet him," Popcorn whispered so softly that we could barely hear him above the sounds of the bus. "I need to talk to him about the number one fan."

"Oh," I whispered.

"Seat twelve!" Mrs. Blanky barked from the front of the bus. "No talking!"

We rode along in silence for another few minutes. I heard some gulping sounds and weird breathing, so I turned my head. Popcorn was actually crying. On the bus!

For some reason this kind of annoyed me. "It's not that big a deal, Popcorn," I said in a voice a little louder and a little meaner than I'd intended. "It's not anything to cry about."

"Leave him alone, Oliver," Brain whisper-warned. She leaned forward and looked across Popcorn at me. "It's not his fault. It's my mom's fault."

It's really my *mom's fault, though*, I thought. *She's the one who left my dad, and if she hadn't left him, maybe he would've stayed in Virginia and never gone to Florida to work for Walker Stewart. Or maybe it's Carl's fault. I don't know. It's someone's.*

"This whole thing was a stupid idea," I whispered to

Brain, or to Popcorn, or maybe to myself. It was completely stupid to think that I could meet Tito the Bonecrusher and rescue my dad from jail.

"Hey, it was *my* idea," Brain hissed, "and it wasn't stupid."

"Why have you been helping me, anyway?" I whispered back.

"Because you're my *friend*," Brain snapped.

The bus screeched to a halt. Then we heard Mrs. Blanky's terrifying voice.

"SEAT TWELVE! YOU ARE IN VIOLATION OF RULES SEVEN AND TWENTY-THREE! THIS IS YOUR LAST WARNING!"

Brain and I pressed our spines completely against the back of the seat and stared ahead.

The bus started moving again.

I was about to grumble some sort of apology at Popcorn, just to get Brain off my back, when he whispered something else.

"I'm . . . Tito . . . fan . . ."

He whispered so super softly, I felt like I had to turn my ears inside out to catch any of it. But I figured I had a good idea of what he was probably saying. He was a fan of Tito, so he really wanted to meet him. But he had no idea how much more important it was to *me*. Tito was my only hope, because he was the only person who cared enough about helping people to want to help me, and he was the only person who would know *how* to help me. And some bad, bone-buzzing feelings started to come up from where I'd pushed them down, and some voice inside said maybe Tito *couldn't* help me. Maybe my dad really was going to be stuck in Florida for years. In prison. He wouldn't be able to come to Virginia for Louisa's graduation, even though he'd promised he would. And maybe Louisa would never forgive him. The buzzing got stronger, and it was in me everywhere, like a roller-coaster drop that goes on too long, where the fun part is over and you're just shaking and falling and wishing you were back on the sidewalk. I covered my ears and closed my eyes.

I think I might have yelled or something, because the next thing I knew, the bus SCREECHED to a halt again.

"SEAT TWELVE. EXIT."

I heard Mrs. Blanky pull the lever to open the door.

I looked up. Brain and Popcorn were eyeing me carefully. Probably because I had just screamed on the bus.

"SEAT TWELVE," Mrs. Blanky repeated.

"She's kidding," Brain whispered. "She's not actually going to make us walk home."

Brain didn't look like she believed what she was saying, though.

"*NOW,*" Blanky barked.

Little Joey in the seat in front of us started to cry. Brain, Popcorn, and I grabbed our backpacks. All the other kids stared at us in shocked silence as we marched down the aisle and down the steps of the bus.

Mrs. Blanky closed the door and drove away. We had been let off right in front of the Fluff Cream Dairy Dessert Shop, at the corner of Culverton and Main. Mr. Jiggly Fluff was standing on the sidewalk in front of the store, holding a sign that said FREE WAFFLE CONE WITH PURCHASE.

Getting kicked off the bus wasn't the greatest—it was super cloudy and cold for May, plus I'm not big on exercise—but at least now we could figure out what the heck Popcorn had been talking about.

"What the heck were you talking about?" I asked him, glancing at Mr. Jiggly Fluff to see if our conversation was being overheard.

"Um, well, I haven't really . . . I haven't told anyone this, but you know that letter that Tito got from a kid a few years back? The one that said it was from his number one fan?"

Was this a serious question? Brain and I had probably

123

talked about Tito on the bus in front of Popcorn every day so far this year, except for the day we got distracted by the mailbox crash.

"You *know* we know," Brain said. "What about it?"

"I, basically, I kind of wrote it," Popcorn said.

"You mean you wrote a letter like it?" I clarified.

"Well, no," Popcorn said. "I mean, I wrote the letter."

"Not really, though," I said. "I mean, not the one that says 'Dear Tito, I love to watch your movies. You are so exciting . . .'"

"Yeah, that's the one," Popcorn said. He looked kind of nervous.

"Whoa," Brain said, a little dazed.

"Wait, so you're saying . . . YOU'RE the number one FAN?"

This was not possible. One day Brain and I had spent about four hours reading message boards where people tried to piece together clues about the number one fan. Lots of folks thought he was one of Tito's relatives in Mexico. Some people believed Tito made him up. Nobody thought he was some kid squished in the middle of seat twelve on bus 179.

"Yeah," Popcorn said.

"But your dad is a famous writer," I said. "You're rich."

"He hasn't always been famous," Popcorn responded, kicking at the leaves on the sidewalk.

Mr. Jiggly Fluff shouted something at us.

"Let's walk," I said, moving as quickly as I could and avoiding eye contact as I passed Mr. Jiggly Fluff. Then I turned the corner and hustled down Culverton Avenue.

Brain and Popcorn followed. I didn't slow down until we were out of sight of Mr. Jiggly Fluff and the Fluff Cream store.

As we made our way slowly down Culverton Avenue toward Brain's house, Popcorn told us about how he had written his fan letter to Tito in third grade.

"I didn't know that my teacher had mailed it," Popcorn said. "Then I heard about it on the news. The video of Tito reading my letter was everywhere."

"But why didn't you tell anyone?" I asked. I figured if I were Popcorn, I would have been bragging to everyone that I was Tito's number one fan and he had talked about me at SmashFest.

"It's embarrassing," Popcorn said. "I said all that stuff about my dad and not being able to pay rent."

"Hey! You got a hundred thousand dollars from Fists O'Blarney!" For a moment, I had forgotten about the bet between Fists and Tito.

"No, I didn't," Popcorn said. "I don't know what happened. I guess maybe it took so long for Tito to get the money from Fists O'Blarney that he couldn't find us."

"That's just like O'Blarney," Brain said bitterly.

"Yeah, and that was around the time my dad sold his book for a lot of money, so we moved to a new apartment and then to our house."

"What did your dad say about the letter?" Brain asked.

"Nothing. He doesn't know about it. We don't really talk to each other that much."

"But you see each other every day!" I exclaimed. It was so strange to me that someone could have their dad nearby and not talk to him.

"I mean, we talk to each other," Popcorn said, "but mostly about writing. And mostly it's my dad talking to me."

"I get it," Brain said.

"Where's your mom?" I asked.

Popcorn shrugged. "I don't know."

"Oh," I said. I wasn't sure what else to ask about that.

"Also, my dad doesn't like wrestling or action movies," Popcorn continued. "He says the storytelling is woefully base."

"Oh," I said again, nodding like I knew what that meant.

By this point we were in front of Brain's house. The three of us trudged up her walk and through the front door. We collected our snacks in silence. I was in shock. If Tito's number one fan was in my bus seat, it seemed like a sign that I was meant to meet Tito and find out how to save my dad.

"I feel like there's something we're missing," Brain mused as we sat in her rec room. She hadn't even bothered to get her homework out yet. "Some other way to never quit trying."

"We could use fake money to buy the tickets," I suggested. "Fake money that looks real. Counterfeit bills, like in *Coyote Willis: Pioneer Cop*."

"Where could we get fake money that looks real?" Popcorn asked.

"I don't know," I said. "I'm just brainstorming."

"The counterfeiters get thrown in jail for life in *Coyote Willis*," Brain reminded me.

"Maybe your stepdad will give you the money," Popcorn suggested.

Brain and I had already ruled that out for sure. A long time ago, Mom had said that Louisa and I were never allowed to ask Carl for money, and she made Carl promise to tell her if we did. This was part of Mom's big conversation with Louisa and me before she married Carl because

127

she thought the two of us would be all traumatized by moving into Carl's fancy neighborhood. (Never mind that I'd been spending most of my free time at Brain's since I was a little kid.) A bunch of it was Mom reminding us that we are just as good and important as anyone who is rich, we should be proud of who we are, pep talk stuff like that.

"I'm not allowed to ask Carl for money," I told Popcorn.

Brain started scribbling on a piece of paper. I started wishing there was no rule about asking Carl for money. But Mom wanted us to appreciate the "value of a dollar." That's why Louisa had an after-school job.

Louisa's after-school job.

A weird combination of excitement and dread filled me. I knew how we could get into the gala.

"Brain?" I said. "The sponsors!"

Brain stopped writing abruptly. "YES," she declared. "That is a *great* idea. Perfect."

"What sponsors?" Popcorn asked.

"Fluff Cream and Designer Mart," Brain answered. "The web page for the Number One Fan Foundation Gala says that there will be special guests from each sponsor. And the special guest from Fluff Cream has to be Mr. Jiggly Fluff. That's it, Oliver! That's how we'll get you into the gala!" Brain's face was all lit up.

"Maybe," I said. My dread was overtaking my excitement.

"I don't get it," Popcorn said. "How can Mr. Jiggly Fluff help us?"

"Because Mr. Jiggly Fluff is my sister," I said. "Louisa."

★ 14 ★

SECOND-BIGGEST SECRET

"Maybe there's another way," I said. "I don't even know for sure if Louisa is going to be working at the gala," I said.

But even as I said it, I realized I did know. The other day I'd been half listening while Louisa complained to Mom about having to work this coming Saturday night while her friends were going to some "party" that just sounded like a bunch of kids sitting around in a house.

"And even if she is going, I don't know how she could get us in," I added. "Let's think of something else. Forget I mentioned it."

"No, this is going to work," Brain said. "Louisa can sneak you in. Her costume is in a big box, right?" She crumpled up the piece of paper she had been writing on and tossed it in the direction of the trash can, then immediately began writing on the next page of her notepad.

"We'll probably need to get some surveillance equipment," she said, "like in *Time Crusher 2*. When Lance Knightfox is sneaking into the space dungeon and Blade Hogan sits in the space van with TV monitors in it, and he's talking to Lance through an earpiece . . ." Brain was scribbling on her notepad like crazy.

"I don't think we can afford to buy a van," Popcorn worried.

"Well, of course, your surveillance equipment won't be that elaborate," Brain clarified. "But we can probably get you *some* kind of equipment."

Brain loves gadgets. She has a bunch of them, like a little voice recorder and a tiny camera on a keychain.

I was excited about the surveillance equipment, but I still didn't understand one thing. "Why do you keep saying *you*? Can't we *all* go now that we don't need tickets?"

"You will go, Spaghetti-O," Brain said, consulting the latest page on her notepad, "because you have to talk to Tito and find out how to get someone out of a federal correctional center. And Popcorn will go because we made a deal. But we need someone on the outside to make sure this operation goes smoothly. That'll be me."

"Someone on the outside," Popcorn repeated, nodding. "While we're on the inside."

Oh, right. I remembered how we were supposed to get

on the inside. "My sister will never agree to help us," I told them. "I can't tell her we're trying to help Dad. It's like she hates him right now."

Brain put her notebook down. "Maybe we can tell her about Popcorn," she said. "And if that doesn't work . . ." Brain looked from side to side over her shoulders, like someone might be listening in. She lowered her voice. "I don't love having to do this, but we can use signature move number four. We know Louisa's biggest secret, and we can threaten to tell people that she's Mr. Jiggly Fluff."

Actually, Louisa's biggest secret was that Dad was in prison. I was pretty sure she hadn't told any of her friends.

But being Mr. Jiggly Fluff was still a big secret. Louisa didn't want anyone to know that she has an after-school job, let alone that she's Mr. Jiggly Fluff.

"You said her name is Louisa?" Popcorn asked, giving me a funny look. "Louisa Jones, right?"

I nodded.

"I bet she'll help us," Popcorn said.

"You don't know her," I told him. But it's not like we had a bunch of other options. I checked the time. It was after five, which meant Louisa would be home from work any minute. "Let's go ahead and get this over with."

We marched down the stairs, out the door, and across the grass to my house.

LOUISA

Louisa was already downstairs in the TV room, lying on the couch and watching *Los Angeles High*, this show about high schoolers who like surfing and hanging out at a diner. It is the most pointless, boring show I have ever seen, but Louisa loves it almost as much as Brain's mom loves her reality shows. I knew Louisa wouldn't be happy that I was interrupting *Los Angeles High*, especially if I was interrupting it to ask for something.

Popcorn, Brain, and I stood beside the TV, and I began a little speech I'd made up in my head on the way over, explaining why Popcorn needed to meet Tito.

I'd gotten only as far as "of the utmost importance that you help us" when Louisa held up her hand to stop me.

"Forget it," she said, her eyes never leaving the TV. "Go away."

Clearly, Louisa was in a terrible mood. My nice little

speech was not going to work. We had to go right for the throat and use signature move #4.

"Louisa, if you don't do it, I'm going to tell everyone that you are Mr. Jiggly Fluff," I proclaimed.

"Whatever," Louisa said, sounding as bored as the kids on her beloved *Los Angeles High*.

"I mean it, Louisa," I said. "Everyone at school will know. Everyone."

A look of absolute shock crossed her face. I thought maybe my threat had gotten through to her. But no.

"Oh my gosh, I have that *same* nail polish!" she squealed, pointing at a character on the screen.

All of a sudden the TV went dark.

"HEY!" Louisa gave me a death stare. "TURN IT BACK ON, Spaghetti-O."

"I didn't do anything!" I argued.

I glanced around and saw that Popcorn had grabbed the remote. He stood in front of Louisa.

"Louisa, please help us," he said sweetly. "I want to meet Tito the Bonecrusher."

"Who the heck are you?" she asked, then grabbed for the remote. "Actually, I don't care who you are. Turn my TV BACK ON."

I saw Popcorn clench his fist around the remote. He took a deep breath. "Louisa, please help us or I'm going to tell my babysitter that you are Mr. Jiggly Fluff."

"Oooh, your *baby*sitter," Louisa said.

Brain and I looked at each other. Whatever Popcorn was doing, it wasn't part of the plan.

"My babysitter is Mitzy Calhoun," Popcorn said. His voice was steely.

I had heard the name Mitzy Calhoun many, many times. If they made an action movie of Louisa's quest to be the valedictorian of Haselton High, then Mitzy Calhoun would be the villain. Mitzy has been Louisa's mortal enemy since tenth grade, when she asked to see one of Louisa's already-graded lab reports, and then she pointed out to the teacher that Louisa's grade had been miscalculated and should have been three points lower.

Mitzy would be the last person Louisa would ever want to know about Mr. Jiggly Fluff, and somehow Popcorn had known this. I guessed that when Mitzy was babysitting, she had the same number of nice things to say about Louisa as Louisa had to say about her. Which would be a total of zero.

Popcorn wanted to make his threat perfectly clear. "As you know, Mitzy plans to be a famous journalist when she grows up. She hosts the morning news at Haselton High, and she told me every homeroom watches it. I'm sure she would be very interested to know that you are Mr. Jiggly Fluff."

Popcorn's words seemed to have struck real fear into

Louisa's cold, bored heart. She narrowed her eyes. "You wouldn't."

"Not if you help us," Popcorn's voice was sweet again.

Now Louisa was listening. Popcorn, Brain, and I took turns explaining the details of the plan, including how Popcorn and I would hide in the Mr. Jiggly Fluff costume box, then sneak into the gala.

"Then what?" Louisa asked.

"Then . . . we're at the gala," I repeated.

Louisa explained to us in the meanest way possible that just because we got into the gala didn't mean we were in the clear. "It's a seated *dinner*," she said, like we were so clueless we were embarrassing her. "The plates are *assigned*. If you don't have a place at a table, they're going to know right away that you don't belong. Each place setting has a little place card with the person's name on it."

"Maybe we could make our own place cards," I offered.

"And what else? Bring your own chairs and plates?" Louisa sneered. "I'm telling you, there won't be anywhere for you to sit. Nancy Dunston is coordinating the whole event, and she'll know if even one fork is out of place."

"Nancy Dunston?" Brain echoed, her voice faint.

"Isn't that Sharon's mom?" Popcorn exclaimed.

Sharon Dunston.

Our plan for meeting Tito the Bonecrusher was going to involve that two-faced priss Sharon Dunston? She had landed me in the headmaster's office twice, and that was nothing compared to what she had done to Brain.

But for me, this wasn't about Sharon, or Brain. It was about being the only person who could rescue my dad. I would never quit trying, and I knew that Brain and Popcorn wouldn't, either. We had already made a deal with Louisa. We could deal with Sharon.

"Brain," I began.

"Nope," she said.

"Brain—"

"Don't wanna hear it." She covered her ears.

Popcorn looked back and forth between us. Louisa had returned to her TV show.

"Let's go upstairs," I said. Popcorn and Brain followed me.

As I walked upstairs, I thought about what Brain had said to me earlier, about Tito sometimes having to work with people he doesn't like so he can get his own way. Then I thought about the scene in *Steel Cage 2: Back in the Cage* when Bruce Paxton tells his partner Leroy (played by The Germ, of course) that they have to work with their former enemy Rosco Jones to break Bruce Paxton's mother out of the science laboratory, because Rosco is the custodian at the laboratory and has all the keys. Bruce Paxton stands up and says to Leroy, "Leroy, here's some science for you: I don't care if I have to make a deal with the cuss-word devil himself, I'm getting the keys to that laboratory." It's like the second-most-famous quote from *Steel Cage 2*, after "Bruce Paxton always saves the day—even when it's night."

I closed the door to my room, took a deep breath, and prepared to quote Bruce Paxton's speech to Brain. I was ready to do whatever it would take to convince Brain that we could do this. She had been pushing us forward, and now it was my turn.

"Brain," I declared. My voice kind of broke, so I cleared my throat and started again. "Brain, here's some science for you: I don't care if I have to make a deal—"

"I know," she groaned before I could even finish the quote. "We have to talk to Sharon."

SHARON

Brain, Popcorn, and I walked the two doors down to Sharon's house and huddled together shoulder to shoulder. It was still cold and had started to rain, and "Grab a jacket!" hadn't been part of Bruce Paxton's speech to Leroy, so we were just shivering on the porch.

All of the houses in my new neighborhood are extremely nice, but Sharon's has an extra layer of fanciness. Her door has all these squiggly designs carved into it, and the glass windows on either side of her door look like something you might see in a church, with shapes and flowers etched into them.

I rang the doorbell. We waited.

I saw movement out of the corner of my eye.

I took two steps to the right and looked through the etched pane of glass to see Sharon's face staring back at me.

"What do you want?" Her voice was muffled and her

face was distorted through the flowery glass, but I could see that she was seriously frowning.

"We need to talk to you," I said.

"About what?" she asked, still muffled.

I looked at Brain, who was looking madder by the second, probably because Sharon wasn't opening the door and we were left out on her porch. "We need your help," I said.

"Why should I help *you*?"

"Because . . . ," I began. I had hoped to talk to Sharon directly. As I'd learned from Tito's movies, people have a harder time saying no to you when you're face-to-face. "Because we need to—"

"Oh, for the love of money, open the cuss-word door, Sharon," Brain interrupted, stepping in front of me to lean her face close to the glass. "We're freezing out here. Popcorn's with us, and he's about to become a Pop*sicle*."

This was true. Popcorn's teeth were chattering.

Sharon's face disappeared from behind the glass pane, and then the door opened. She smiled sweetly. "Come on in, Paul," she said to Popcorn, who stepped inside. Then she crossed her arms, stared at Brain and me for a moment, and smirked. "You have to say the password."

This seemed like a trap. "What's the password?" I asked.

"The password is," she announced, "WE ARE SORRY, SHARON."

I grabbed Brain by the elbow before she could run off the porch or punch Sharon in the face.

"Can the password be something else?" I asked. "Like 'open sesame' or something? You got me sent to Saturday Service Reflection." (I didn't bother to mention that Popcorn had taken my place.) "I'm not going to say sorry."

Sharon smirked again and opened her mouth to say something else, but I kept going.

"And Brain's not going to say sorry, either, after what you said about her."

Sharon's face turned kind of pink. "I didn't say anything about Brain."

"Don't lie, Sharon," Brain growled beside me.

So I guess I should back up and explain how everything broke down with Sharon, Brain, and me over the summer. Like I said, I used to hang out at Brain's house on Saturdays while my mom was working. Sharon would come over, and we would play these games that Brain invented.

For a while we used to play a game that Brain called Crime Scan. The idea was that we would patrol the neighborhood looking for criminal activity. But my mom said we were allowed no farther than the end of Brain's driveway, so we did most of our crime scanning from her front yard. The only crimes we saw were people running the stop sign at the corner of Culverton and First, or not picking up their dog's poop when they were out walking. Also the across-the-street neighbors almost never cut their grass, but we weren't sure that was a crime, even if Brain's dad complained about it a lot. Even though there wasn't a lot of crime, Sharon took notes and shared them with her mom, who was in charge of the Neighborhood Watch, whatever that was.

When we weren't playing Crime Scan, we played in Brain's backyard playhouse. The playhouse had been decorated by Brain's mom with fuzzy pink beanbag chairs, purple shutters that really opened and closed, and a pastel play kitchen. It also had Barbies everywhere, which was great because Brain invented this game called Barbie Attack and we needed a bunch of Barbies for it.

Here's how to play Barbie Attack: One kid is outside the playhouse, and the other kids are inside the playhouse with the shutters open. The outside kid has to run circles around the playhouse, and the inside kids throw Barbies through the open windows. The inside kids get a point every time they hit the outside kid with a Barbie.

It's rough on the Barbies, but none of us really cared except for Sharon.

"Can't we just play regular Barbies?" Sharon asked one day. "Or house?"

"No," Brain declared.

Brain could be kind of bossy to Sharon, but I didn't care because I sure as heck didn't want to play Barbies, either.

"We can play wrestling with the Barbies," I suggested.

"Okay," Sharon said.

We pretended that Totally Hair Barbie was Tito the Bonecrusher and Prom Night Barbie was John Rancid. We also used Malibu Skipper as The Germ. We drew on Totally Hair Barbie's face with dry-erase markers because it's pretty much impossible to find a store that sells lucha libre masks for Barbies, no matter how many places you ask. We borrowed a chair from Barbie's Dream House to perform John Rancid's signature move of smashing a chair over Tito's head. Tito went down hard and the referee (Wedding Day Ken) started counting, "One, two . . . ," and then Tito got up and started to fight again.

"Let's keep going till one of their arms pops off," I suggested.

"This is boring," Sharon complained. "I'm going home if you don't play something else."

"Okay, see you Monday," Brain said.

"See you next week," I added.

"Oh. Okay," Sharon said. Then she left.

I guess that was when it started to change from being me, Brain, and Sharon as best friends to me and Brain as best friends and Sharon as our third best friend. It wasn't like we weren't all friends anymore, we just weren't playing all day every Saturday. I didn't really notice it at first, because there was other stuff going on, like Mom and Carl getting married. But Sharon started spending less and less time with us on Saturdays, and when she did, she kept wanting to do more stuff Brain didn't want to do, like paint her nails or practice cheers that she learned from her cousin.

One Saturday last summer, Sharon brought over this magazine with a bunch of guys on the cover from this cheesy band called 5 Summer Boys, and she asked Brain to take some quiz called "Which Member of 5 Summer Boys Should You Marry?"

"I'm not marrying one of those cheeseballs," Brain scoffed. She was really cranky with Sharon that day. She was spending every weekday with Sharon at day camp, too, and that was enough to make anyone cranky.

"They're not cheeseballs! They're so hot! I think Beau Masters is the hottest. I would marry him. Maybe I will!" Then she made this strange giggle-shrieking sound. "I'm totally going to marry Beau Masters."

"Can I see that?" I asked. I have to admit I was completely fascinated by these extra-shiny magazines of Sharon's. I started flipping through it while Brain and Sharon started arguing.

"Don't be a blockhead, Sharon," Brain said. "You're not going to marry Beau Masters. Let's go outside and play Barbie Attack or something instead of making yourself even cheesier by reading those weird magazines."

I looked up from some magazine quiz questions ("Which of the 5 Summer Boys loves mangoes?" "5 Summer Boys: Why are there 5 of them?") to see that Sharon's face was getting red and her chin was a little wobbly.

"They're not weird!" Sharon cried. "Just because you don't like something doesn't mean it's cheesy and weird. You're the weird one for not liking any girl stuff. And don't call me a blockhead!" Sharon looked at me for some reason, even though Brain was the one who had called her a blockhead. Her eyes were all watery with tears.

"Whatever, Sharon," Brain said, sounding bored. Now she was looking at me, too. "You're not READING that stupid magazine, are you, Oliver?"

"Um, no?" I said, pushing it back toward Sharon. "I don't want to read about those cheeseballs."

Sharon grabbed it. Her tears were spilling over and running down her cheeks. "You're both jerks," she said.

"What did I do?" I said.

"You always agree with *her*!" Now she was flinging tears everywhere. "You're supposed to be *my* friend, too!" Sharon grabbed her magazine and her purse that she carried around for no reason and she stormed out of Brain's house.

I figured she and Brain would work things out at their day camp, but by Saturday things were way worse. According to Brain, Sharon said a bunch of horrible stuff about Brain to some mean girls, and we could never, ever be friends with her again. We spent a couple of weeks talking about all the things that had always annoyed us about Sharon, and it turned out that she had been awful all along and neither of us had really noticed until we took the time to think about it.

Whenever we saw Sharon during the rest of the summer, like at the pool or around the neighborhood, we made a big deal out of ignoring her, and she made a big deal out of ignoring us.

Brain's mom didn't seem to notice that Sharon wasn't hanging out with us anymore, but my mom realized it right away. I think Sharon's mom had called her and said Sharon was upset about it or something.

"It's not a big deal," I told Mom when she asked me what was going on.

"It's a big deal to Sharon," Mom said. But I told her I didn't want to talk about it, and she didn't force me. She just said that although I didn't have to be best friends with Sharon, I should at least be polite.

I tried to be as polite as I could to Sharon without irritating Brain, which wasn't easy since all three of us wound up in Mrs. Thumbly's class when school started. I'd say I was polite about 75 percent of the time, which I thought was pretty good.

The politeness lasted until the first day after winter break, when I saw Sharon in the hallway before class.

"Oliver!" she shrieked, giving me a hug in front of what felt like a thousand people. "I heard about your dad! I'm soooo sorry! I can't believe he might be—"

Then she said it.

"—GOING TO JAIL!"

And, I swear she said it louder than someone could holler it with a microphone. In front of a ton of people. What kind of person does that?

I backed out of her hug. "Don't be a blockhead, Sharon," I said, knowing how much she hated being called a blockhead. "My dad's not going to jail. Quit making up stuff to get attention."

Sharon looked around. She seemed to actually care who was listening, now that she was done blabbing my personal business. "But my mom told me that he was charged with fraud—"

"Your mom's a liar."

You shouldn't call someone's mom a liar, especially when it turns out she's not lying, but I didn't know at the time that it was true.

"*You're* the liar!" Sharon's voice sounded all wobbly. "I wish you'd never come to this school!"

Then she flounced away and, I guess, proceeded to think of all the things she could do to make my life, and Brain's life, impossible.

So that's everything that had happened with Brain, Sharon, and me. Yet there we were on her doorstep, begging for her help. And I'm sure she was absolutely loving it until we brought up her gossiping about Brain over the summer. Now Sharon started apologizing.

"I didn't say you don't like boys," Sharon told Brain. Brain's face turned bright pink. "I said that you didn't like any of the boys in *5 Summer Boys*, and I thought that was weird. I only said it because we were in a fight."

Brain's face was turning redder and redder. "Then why did people tell me you said it?" she demanded. "And what difference does it make who I like or don't like?"

Popcorn, who hadn't known any of this dramatic stuff, didn't seem to know where to look. He looked at Brain, then at Sharon, then at me, and finally stared at the floor.

"Madison said it," Sharon cried. Madison is this annoying friend of Sharon's from summer camp. "Madison said you don't like boys, and I laughed. That's all. I just laughed. I didn't say it."

I imagined what it was like for Brain to hear people at camp whispering and laughing about her.

"I'm sorry I laughed," Sharon went on. "It's been weighing on my heart, Brianna. But we were in a fight! You had been so mean to me! Remember when you said—"

Brain stepped into the house and Sharon stepped aside, forgetting to block our entry. I followed Brain.

"We don't have time to rehash every bad thing we've ever said or done to each other," Brain declared. "You've acted like a jerk, but we need your help, so let's make a deal. What'll it take for you to help us?"

"First tell me what you want me to do," Sharon said, crossing her arms.

"No way," Brain said, crossing her arms right back and staring Sharon down like they were in the wrestling ring. "If we are going to trust you with our most important plan ever, you have to decide whether or not to help us before you have the details."

"No deal." Sharon's voice had turned prissy again.

"Okay, never mind. Let's go, boys," Brain said.

I acted like I was about to head out the door, even though I knew Brain was bluffing. Sharon was way too interested in knowing everyone's business to let us walk away.

At least that's what I'd thought. I was getting closer to the door, and Sharon hadn't given in. I started moving like I was in slow motion, trying to buy some time. As much as Brain hated it, we needed Sharon for this plan to work.

Brain knew it, too. "I'm sorry if I was mean to you, too," she muttered.

Sharon started acting like she and Brain had been reunited after fifty years of separation. "I forgive you, Brianna," she cried. "And I'll help you, on one condition."

"What do you want?" Brain asked.

"I want you to let me come over to your house on Saturdays again," Sharon sniffled.

"Fine," I said before Brain could say no.

"FINE," Brain said through gritted teeth, marching toward Sharon's bedroom so we could lay out the plan.

We told Sharon why Popcorn and I needed to meet Tito and what Louisa had said about the gala being highly organized, and we explained what we needed from her.

She said that, yes, she could get on her mom's computer and change the seating chart. "But it'll have to be at the absolute last minute," she said in her prissiest voice. "Otherwise she'll notice."

We started to talk about some of the other details of the plan, but Sharon started giving us her opinions, which made Brain want to leave. Once we were safely outside, Brain, Popcorn, and I planned to meet again the next day to finalize the details of the operation.

★ 17 ★

I'M PAUL ROBARDS

The next meeting was at Popcorn's house.
Brain's mom had a bunch of ladies over, and my mom
advised us to meet somewhere other than our house since
Louisa was studying for a huge test that could make or
break her battle against Mitzy Calhoun. If we disturbed
her, she might actually end us.

I had never been in Popcorn's house before. It was
smaller than the other houses in the neighborhood, and it
was filled with books—not just on the bookshelves but
also on the floor, on the coffee table, and on one end of
the couch. Little scraps of paper, notebooks, and magazines
were stacked on top of the piles of books. None of the magazines
had famous people's pictures on them.

There was something strange about Popcorn's living
room. I couldn't figure out what it was, exactly, but it made
me feel uneasy.

"Where's your TV?" Brain asked.

That was it.

Popcorn looked around like someone might be listening. "It's in the basement," he half whispered. "My dad doesn't like for visitors to see it. He says it's an ugly but necessary evil in the age of information."

"Uh, okay," I said.

"I'm sorry you have to come home to an empty house," Sharon piped up in this sticky-sweet voice as she snooped around the papers and books in Popcorn's living room. She'd found out we were meeting and insisted on coming with us to Popcorn's house even though we didn't need her for this part.

"Oh, my dad is here," Popcorn said. "He's writing."

Just then there was a loud *bang-clack* from behind a door. Sharon screamed. It's a good thing she wasn't going to be sneaking into the gala with us. She's very jumpy.

"That's my dad's typewriter," Popcorn said. "He writes in a closet without the internet."

"Why?" I asked.

"So the noise of daily life doesn't drown out the truth of his words."

"That's beautiful," Sharon said.

"Huh?" I didn't get it.

"I mean, so he doesn't get distracted and go on Facebook and stuff," Popcorn clarified.

The door where the sound had come from opened, and Popcorn's dad emerged. I sort of recognized him from interviews on the boring public television channel Carl likes to watch.

He squinted in our direction. "Who are you?" he asked. He looked at each of us, making a wrinkled-up face at me. Probably admiring my Tito the Bonecrusher shirt. I have several.

"I'm Sharon Francesca Dunston," Sharon said, and she actually curtsied. "It's a pleasure to meet you, Mr. Robards."

"Dad, these are my friends from school," Popcorn informed him.

"You mean your classmates," Popcorn's dad said. "'Wishing to be friends is quick work, but friendship is a slow-ripening fruit.' The wisdom of Aristotle. You may offer orange juice or milk to your classmates." Popcorn's dad gave us a half nod, went back into his closet, and shut the door.

The *bang-clack*ing started again.

"So that's my dad . . . ," Popcorn said, trailing off.

We got our milk and orange juice and headed up to Popcorn's bedroom. It was the neatest kid's room I had ever seen—even neater than Brain's. I asked Popcorn if he had a housekeeper, but he said no, he just liked to keep things in order in case anyone stopped by.

"Do people stop by a lot?" I asked him.

"Not really," Popcorn said.

"I think it's so very important to be tidy," Sharon said. She was perched on the edge of Popcorn's desk chair with her ankles crossed like she was at a tea party.

"Why are you here, again?" Brain asked her.

"If I'm going to participate in this scheme, I need to be involved in the planning," Sharon snapped.

"Thank you for helping us, Sharon," Popcorn said. "I really appreciate it."

Popcorn was really good at signature move #2: **Be extra friendly**.

"Oh, Paul," Sharon said in this gooey voice like a kindergarten teacher. "I've been meaning to tell you that I think it's wonderful how you expressed your feelings in that letter to Tito."

"We don't have time for feelings, Sharon," Brain said, thank goodness. "We need to finalize the details of the operation." She was lying on the floor of Popcorn's room with her little notebook in hand.

"So, Sharon, if you're getting us place cards for the dinner, can't you get us on the list to come in the front door?" I asked. "Then we won't have to deal with Louisa at all," I said, turning to Brain.

"You can't just come in the front *door*," Sharon said,

like I'd said we wanted to parachute in through the roof. "The security at the front door is being handled by the Empire Hotel. My mom doesn't do *security*, Oliver. You'll have to come in with Louisa. All I can do is add you to the seating chart without my mom noticing."

I know it seems like I should give Sharon credit for using signature move #3, **Take what you need without anyone noticing**, but the whole plan was really Brain's idea, and Sharon was just following through because we made a deal with her.

"I am going to add you to the list on the day of the gala," Sharon continued. "Not under your real names, of course. I am going to give you aliases."

I asked Sharon if we could choose our own aliases, but she said no.

Then we started talking about what we would say to Tito the Bonecrusher.

"I'm going to say, 'I will be CRUSHED if I can't get your help,'" I declared. I thought Tito would like it if I creatively used part of his name to ask for his help. He would explain to me how to rescue my dad, and then I would be ready to go to Florida and save him.

Then Brain asked what Popcorn would say to Tito. "Are you going to come right out and say, 'It's me, your number one fan!'?"

"Oh, I don't know," Popcorn said. "I might get too nervous to say anything."

Sharon patted Popcorn's shoulder and clucked like a mother hen. "That's understandable," she said in the gooey voice.

Wait, what? Popcorn was going to sneak into the gala just to meet Tito, and then he wasn't even going to mention that he was Tito's number one fan?

"That's not understandable! That's ridiculous," I said.

"Yeah," Brain said, and nodded. "You have to tell him. Let's practice. Pretend I'm Tito. What would you say?"

"I don't know." Popcorn looked down and mumbled as fast as he could, "I guess, 'HiMisterTheBonecrusherI'm YourNumberOneFan.'"

"I couldn't understand anything you said," I informed him.

"Try again, but say it more slowly," Brain encouraged.

"Hi, Mr. The Bonecrusher," Popcorn mumbled more slowly, "I'm Paul Robards. I wrote the letter. I'm your number one fan." His voice was barely above a whisper.

"I think when you're talking to him, you call him just 'Tito,' not 'Mr. The Bonecrusher,'" Sharon pointed out.

"And that was still way too quiet," I added.

"Try it as loud as you can," Brain prompted. "You can do it! No one is listening but us!"

"HI, MR. THE BONECRUSHER—I MEAN, TITO," Popcorn began, then closed his eyes tight. "I CAME TO THIS GALA JUST SO I COULD MEET YOU."

"Yeah, there you go!" Brain approved.

"I WROTE YOU A LETTER," he continued hollering. "A LONG TIME AGO. AND TONIGHT WE MEET AT LAST."

This was pretty good. It sounded like some stuff a wrestler would say.

"I'M YOUR NUMBER ONE FAN," he announced. "IT IS I, PAUL ROBARDS!"

I didn't love the ending. "Just say 'It's me,'" I suggested. "'It is I' sounds old-timey."

"'It is I' is correct, though," Brain said.

I was about to argue that none of Tito's characters ever say "It is I" when, suddenly, we heard a lot of commotion from somewhere outside Popcorn's room. The door flew open, and Popcorn's dad was standing there, holding a book.

Popcorn looked utterly panicked.

"Hi, Dad," he said.

Popcorn's dad cleared his throat.

"Paul," he said, stepping inside the room, "what are you going on about?"

"Sorry, Dad. We were just, uh, pretending something."

"Mr. Robards." Sharon clutched her hands to her chest. "We are so sorry to have disturbed your work."

"What were you saying about a gala? And that Tito Bonecrusher fellow?"

"Nothing." Popcorn looked at the floor.

"The best people possess 'the discipline to tell the truth.' The wisdom of Ernest Hemingway."

"Okay," Popcorn said. Then he stood there and said nothing.

"Paul," his dad said again.

"Well," Popcorn began, "there's going to be this gala with Tito the Bonecrusher. I want to go because . . ." He paused. "Because I wrote a letter to Tito. A few years ago."

"And how," Mr. Robards asked coolly, "did a letter lead to the high-volume outburst?"

Popcorn shifted his feet closer together, almost stacking them on top of each other, like he was trying to make himself even smaller than he was. "I asked Tito for help," he mumbled. "So I was going to tell him I was the kid from the letter. I wanted to let him know that I turned out okay, even though he never helped me."

"I see," Popcorn's dad said.

"You two need some privacy," Sharon chirped. She was

off the chair and out the door before Popcorn could say any more.

Brain was right behind her.

I started to follow them, but then I heard Popcorn's quiet voice behind me.

"Can you stay, Oliver?"

"I, uh, okay," I said. I wasn't wild about being in the middle of something between Popcorn and his dad.

I heard muffled talking and some bumps against the door. *Those two are standing right outside*, I thought. I would have done the same thing.

Popcorn's dad was fidgety. He was rubbing his hands together, and he wouldn't look Popcorn in the eye.

"Actually, Paul," he said, "Tito the Bonecrusher *did* help you."

☆ **18** ☆

THE TRUTH ABOUT TITO

Oh.

This was a twist. Like in *Coyote Willis: Pioneer Cop*, when the sheriff turned out to be the counterfeiter that Tito had been trying to find all along.

"He did?" Popcorn was shocked. "Is that why we have this house? Did he pay for it?"

"Not all of it," Popcorn's dad said, sounding offended.

"What else did he do?"

"He . . . knew some people who could help publish my book."

This made sense. Tito has written several bestsellers, including *Never Quit Trying: My Life in the Ring* and *Thyme Crusher: The Tito the Bonecrusher Cookbook*.

"Why didn't you tell me? Were you embarrassed?" Popcorn asked.

His dad made that coughing sound that sometimes

happens when you fake-laugh. "No, of course not. But you have much better things to do with your time than idolize overpaid wrestlers."

"You should have TOLD me, though! It was my letter!" Popcorn's face was getting red.

Now I was really uncomfortable. I started reading the titles of books on Popcorn's shelf as though Popcorn and his dad weren't arguing.

"Look how upset you've become," Popcorn's dad said, getting calmer as Popcorn got angrier—which is a thing my mom does, and it's the worst. "All because of an unhealthy attachment to some celebrity. I don't want to hear any more about Tito the Bonecrusher."

Wow. Popcorn's dad REALLY didn't want Popcorn to be a fan of Tito the Bonecrusher.

It reminded me of *Time Crusher 2: Out of Time*. Tito's character, Lance Knightfox, normally fought crime with his cousin, Blade Hogan (played by The Germ, of course), but he worked with a new guy when his cousin was recovering from a laser injury. Blade worried that Lance liked his new partner better, so he tried to sabotage him.

It occurred to me that maybe Popcorn's dad was worried that Popcorn would like Tito more than him. And that was just silly. Tito was awesome, but he was no substitute for a dad.

"Popcorn will never love Tito as much as he loves you, Mr. Robards," I said. It was just like with Brain's mom. These rich grown-ups sure did need to know people loved them all the time. Mr. Robards looked confused, then annoyed, but I kept talking. "'Ain't no lasers strong enough on this planet to break to bonds of family.' The wisdom of Lance Knightfox."

Mr. Robards looked at me, then at Popcorn, and his face got kind of wobbly as Popcorn hugged him. I watched this for only about a half second before I had some feelings come up that I needed to push down. I hustled to the door and then left with Brain and Sharon.

★ 19 ★

PAUL POPCORN AND
OLIVER SPAGHETTI

Four days later, Mom and Carl thought I
was spending the night at Popcorn's house. Instead, I was
in a box in the women's restroom at the Empire Hotel, trying
not to breathe in Popcorn's pine-tree scent and ignoring
the buzzing in my ear.

Brain, who was supposed to be spending the night at
my house, had gone totally over the top with her job as
"someone on the outside." She wanted me to have an earpiece so she could communicate with Popcorn and me
the way Lance Knightfox talks to Blade Hogan in *Time
Crusher*. We'd thought we could get top-of-the-line spy
gear with our commercial money, but then we found out
that genuine high-tech surveillance equipment is
extremely expensive. So we got this cheap walkie-talkie
and earpiece set from Radio Hut. The set was called Spy
Buddies, and on the box there was a picture of two kids in

sunglasses and trench coats. Underneath the kids it said, REAL SPYING FUN FOR KIDS AGES FOUR AND UP!

There were several problems with the Spy Buddies set. For one thing, the earpiece and walkie-talkie didn't work well if they were far apart. Plus, Brain wasn't going to be in a location where she was going to be able to do any actual spying. She was just going to be sitting on the bench right outside the hotel, holding the walkie-talkie and hoping to see or hear something interesting.

"Why do you smell like pine trees?" I whispered to Popcorn. I was folded up at the bottom of the box, and he was practically sitting on top of me. It was not comfortable. "It's tear-free shampoo," Popcorn answered. "My dad has sensitive eyes from the darkness in his writing closet." Mr. Robards, who was probably in his writing closet at that moment, thought Popcorn was spending the night at my house. Even though he'd given up lecturing us about celebrities and intellectual something or other, it was better for everyone if he didn't get involved in our gala mission.

"*BBZZZZ CH CH CH*, Spaghetti-O? *CHCHCHCH*," I heard in my ear.

"I'm here," I responded, not that Brain could hear me. The other problem with the Spy Buddies set was that I couldn't communicate back to Brain. She was able to talk into my ear, but I had no way to respond.

"I don't know if you can hear *CHCHCHCH*," Brain went on, "but I hope you guys are doing well. Nothing is *CHCH* out here. People are just *CHCHCHCH*."

"What's she saying?" Popcorn asked me.

"I'm not really sure," I told him.

Popcorn shifted his weight, sending his knee farther into my spine.

"Urp!" I tried not to yelp too loud in case anyone else was in the bathroom with Louisa.

"Sorry," Popcorn said. "Both my legs and both my arms are asleep."

We must have been in the box for at least an hour, from the time we'd climbed in at the Jiggly Fluff store, to the bumpy van ride, to the ride on a little wheeled cart past the security line and into the women's restroom. The cart dumped the two boxes on the floor in the extra-large stall, where there would be plenty of room for Louisa to change into the Mr. Jiggly Fluff costume. Louisa had insisted on bringing two boxes. One box had her costume, and the other box was supposed to have a backup costume. But instead of the backup costume, the second enormous box held Popcorn and me.

Louisa was going to let us out of the box when the women's bathroom was empty, but we had been waiting a long time.

"I think Louisa is leaving us in here just to mess with us," I whispered to Popcorn.

Just then I heard a squeak at the top of the box as the hinge opened. I turned my head as much as possible and saw light above.

"Get out," Louisa said flatly. "The coast is clear or whatever."

Popcorn and I tried to get out of the box as quickly as possible, but we had totally stiffened up from being crammed in there for so long.

"Come on," Louisa muttered. "You know one of these rich ladies is going to have to go to the bathroom soon."

"Aaaah!" I heard Popcorn scream as I was trying to drag my numb legs out of the box. I looked around and saw what had made him holler: The head of the Mr. Jiggly Fluff costume was sitting on the floor beside the toilet.

"Sorry," Popcorn whispered. "It surprised me."

Popcorn's hair was sticking up all over the place. His suit was hopelessly wrinkled, and I was sure mine was, too.

"Follow me," Louisa said, sounding as bored as ever.

She led us out of the bathroom stall, pushed open the main door to the bathroom, and glanced from side to side.

"Go," she said.

Popcorn practically ran out the door.

"Well, thanks," I said to Louisa.

"Don't get caught," she said.

I tried to play it cool as I followed Popcorn down the short hallway to the big room where the gala was being held. "Holy moly!" I screeched when I walked into the ballroom. The room was totally sparkly and filled with people.

"Spaghetti-O, *CHCH*," I heard in my ear, "we forgot to talk about your cover *CHCH*." Brain's voice was cutting in and out again. "If anyone asks why you're there, tell them that you're pi-*CHHH*." Her voice was replaced by total static.

Popcorn pointed to the left, where three ladies with fancy hairdos were sitting behind a long table. On the table there were little folded cards with words printed on them. "I think that's where we get our table assignment," Popcorn said.

I followed Popcorn to the table.

"Don't you two boys look so *hand*some!" the lady in the middle said.

Popcorn gawked at her. "Wow, you have a lot of diamonds in your earrings," he said. "They must have been expensive!"

The woman looked a little embarrassed.

"Never mind him," I told her, and gave her this fancy-party smile I had practiced in front of a mirror as part of signature move #1 (**Project confidence**). After moving into Carl's neighborhood and changing schools, I'd learned pretty quickly that talking to a rich person is like facing down a wild bear. If you meet a bear in the woods, you should never act all nervous and skittish, or they'll sniff you out as a human in about two seconds. Instead, you're supposed to stand your ground and act bigger than you are. Then the bear will think you're another bear and leave you alone. Same goes for rich people. You have to either convince them you're one of them or convince them you don't care. You can't act nervous or they'll tear you apart. It can be exhausting, but you want to survive, don't you?

Anyway, I projected confidence and gave our names to the rich ladies. At least, I gave them the names that Sharon had added to the list for the place cards.

"Here you go, Paul Popcorn and Oliver . . . Spaghetti? Well, those are certainly unusual last names," the lady on the left said. "You're both at table seventeen."

"Rich people don't like for you to ask if things are expensive," I advised Popcorn as we walked away from the place-card table. "They think it's tacky to say things are expensive."

"So they want us to think their stuff is cheap?" Popcorn asked. We walked past some tuxedoed guys holding snacks on silver trays, just like in the movies.

"No, you're supposed to know it's expensive but not talk about it." I was surprised Popcorn didn't know this stuff. After all, he goes to Haselton Academy. Then I realized his dad probably wasn't really on the rich-people scene.

"Oh," Popcorn said.

We reached our table. Table 17 was near the back of the ballroom. I had asked Sharon if she could put us at Tito's table or even at the table next to him. "Are you serious?" She had looked at me like I'd asked for a seat in Tito's lap. "That would make it thoroughly obvious that you aren't supposed to be there. They would catch you in about five seconds. I'm putting you at table seventeen, and it's up to you to find Tito and get his autograph."

Popcorn and I decided to put our place cards down at our table before walking around to find Tito. An old lady and an old man were already sitting at table 17. Popcorn and I introduced ourselves. The old lady's name was Gwen, and the old man's name was Something. I didn't really listen to his name because Gwen asked us a question while the old man was introducing himself.

"You look familiar," Gwen said to me. "Do I know you?"

I looked at her carefully. She looked like a standard old lady to me. Gray hair, wrinkles, nice big old-lady smile. "No, ma'am," I said. "I don't think so."

Gwen looked from me to Popcorn. "What brings you here tonight? Are your parents with you, dears?" she said.

"Welllll," I said. I wasn't sure how to answer. I can't believe we hadn't thought about how to answer these kinds of questions. Of course people would wonder why two eleven-year-olds were wandering around a fancy party alone. We should have spent more time thinking about cover stories and less time buying spy equipment at Radio Hut.

Gwen was watching me carefully.

"Oh, our parents *love* Tito the Bonecrusher," I said, which wasn't a lie.

Popcorn stared at Gwen. I'm guessing he didn't know what to add, so I just kept talking.

"What brings *you* here tonight, ma'am?" I asked Gwen.

"*Ma'am!* Don't you have such nice manners?" Gwen beamed at me. "I'm here because my dear friend from the garden club encouraged all of us to buy tickets. She is receiving an award for her charitable donations."

Gwen sounded just like Granny Janet, talking about the garden club and charitable donations. Good grief. They could be best friends.

Wait. *Granny Janet.*

"Um, what's your friend's name from the garden club?" I asked.

171

"Janet Wyatt," Gwen said, and smiled at me. "I thought she would be at this table, but I think she's sitting near the stage."

I stared at Gwen, and my eyes must have been as wide as silver dollars.

She didn't seem to notice. "What grade are you boys in?" she asked.

This time, Popcorn was the one who projected confidence. "It sure is swell to meet you folks," he said, nodding to both Gwen and Something. "Will you excuse us?" He grabbed me by the elbow and pulled me away from the table.

"What's wrong, Spaghetti-O?" he asked me when we were a few tables away.

I finally blinked. "Janet Wyatt is Granny Janet, my step-grandma," I whispered. Between me trying to rescue my dad and Popcorn trying to meet his hero, I had completely forgotten that Granny Janet would be at the gala. I had forgotten, even though Granny Janet was the reason we'd found out about the gala in the first place. "She's here somewhere." I looked around frantically. Where was she? Had she already seen me?

"That's great!" Popcorn brightened. "She can introduce us to Tito!"

"No way!" I hissed. Granny Janet would probably turn us over to the police for trespassing.

I looked toward the tables close to the stage at the front of the ballroom, and it took me only about two seconds to spot Granny Janet. I was surprised I hadn't noticed her before. She was wearing a bright green dress with about a million ruffles, and she had on a little hat with a huge peacock feather sticking up out of it. I turned around so she'd only see my back if she looked in my direction. "She's at the front," I told Popcorn. "In the green dress. And the feather hat."

Popcorn craned his neck. "That's your GRANNY?" he said, amazed.

I nodded.

"Oh wow," Popcorn said. "Okay, let's go find Tito."

"I can't go yet," I told him, my back still to Granny Janet. "I can't let her see me."

Popcorn craned his neck again to look at Granny Janet. "I don't think she'll notice us. It's pretty crowded. We have to go talk to him now."

"Not yet," I repeated.

Popcorn was still looking at Granny Janet. "She's busy talking to someone. Let's go."

I didn't move.

"What are you waiting for?"

I felt the weird itching in my bones. The longer I waited to meet Tito, the longer I could believe he could help me rescue my dad. But once I met him, there was a chance he could say no.

173

I closed my eyes and took a deep breath. He wouldn't say no. Not to his number one fan, and not to a kid who needed help. He would help us. He would say *Never quit trying*. And if I didn't go meet him now, I would miss my chance.

My Spy Buddies earpiece buzzed, but I ignored the *CHCHCH* of Brain's spy report, opened my eyes, turned around, and started marching forward.

Suddenly I was being yanked backward by the collar of my shirt. Popcorn lurched backward, too. We both spun around to find Louisa, not yet in her Mr. Jiggly Fluff costume, glowering at us.

"I just saw Granny Janet at a front table," she proclaimed. "You can't go up there—"

"I know it's risky, but I have to go in," I said. "And if I get caught, we'll never tell anyone you helped us. Your good name is safe." This was word for word the exact speech that Bruce Paxton gives to Rosco Jones in *Steel Cage 2*, but I don't think Louisa remembered that.

"I'm not worried about my good name," Louisa said, rolling her eyes. "I'm trying to save your stupid mission." She looked over our heads and scanned the crowd. "We'll go along the left wall on the other side of Tito's table."

"But the line to meet him is in the middle—"

"We don't need the line." Louisa pushed us toward one

side of the ballroom, then forward along the wall until we were next to a little tree in a giant pot. "Be cool," she said.

She stepped forward toward the circle of people around Tito's table.

"Danger Rick!" she said, waving to a man with a ponytail.

The ponytail man looked up, confused.

Louisa smiled big. "Hey, I just wanted to say how awesome you were in the Summer Shakeup match against Vince Gnash a few years ago. That was one of the top three underrated face turns in the history of UWE. I was disappointed that you didn't join the Triple Diamond Coalition, but I totally respect your decision to step away from the spotlight and go behind the scenes into management. The UWE is sooooo lucky to have you."

"Whoa," I heard Popcorn say.

I hadn't heard Louisa talk wrestling in years. It was like the old Louisa was still in there somewhere, underneath the part that told me to go away all the time.

"Thanks," said Danger Rick, who was apparently some small-time former wrestler who now worked in management for UWE. I had never heard of him, but Louisa had always known a lot more about UWE than I did. I just knew the superstars and the guys who came from lucha libre.

"I am *such* a fan," Louisa gushed. "Can I get an autograph?"

"Yeah, of course," he replied.

Danger Rick exchanged nods with two big guys in suits who were probably bodyguards. They had earpieces that were way more expensive than the junky one in my ear. They waved us forward.

Louisa pulled the gala program out of her purse for Danger Rick to sign. "By the way, we'd love to meet Tito," she added casually.

"Sure," Danger Rick said.

My heart started pounding.

This was it.

"Good evening," a man's voice boomed from the stage. "Welcome to the Number One Fan Foundation Gala. If all of you could please take your seats, we will begin our program with an introduction from the foundation's director."

One of the bodyguard guys muttered something to Danger Rick.

"They're saying we have to take our seats right away," he told Louisa, "but come back later and I will introduce you to Tito."

"Okay," Louisa said, hustling us away. "That sounds great."

The next thing I knew we were out of the circle of people around Tito. Instead we were alongside the wall next to the sad little tree in the giant pot, like we had never been that close to Tito at all.

"Thanks for trying, Louisa," I said. "That was amazing."

"Yeah, whatever," she said, and walked away.

★20★

WE ARE PIONEER COPS

Popcorn and I went back to table 17, where some other people had joined Gwen and Something. Popcorn and I were the last two to sit down. Fortunately, our seats were facing away from the stage. I figured Granny Janet wouldn't recognize the back of my head.

"Are your parents not going to sit with you?" Gwen asked us.

"Uh, they're eating at a different table tonight," I mumbled, which was also technically not a lie.

A bunch of waiters in black-and-white outfits started reaching around people to stick salads in front of them on the table. I took my salad plate from a waiter's hand so he wouldn't have to reach. The plate was freezing! I guess if you pay a lot of money for a salad, they want to make sure it's cold. The salad already had some kind of brown dressing on it. I usually only eat ranch dressing, but I decided not to draw attention to myself by making a big deal about it. I grabbed the biggest of the three forks in front of me and started to eat my salad.

Gwen had more questions for us, though. "I don't see any other children," she said, smiling. "How did you two get the lucky opportunity to come to this gala?"

Jeez, what was with this lady? Was she a secret agent or something?

All that popped into my head was what Brain had said through the earpiece, "Tell them that you're pi-CHCH."

"We are pi . . . We are pi . . ." I tried to think fast about what Brain might have been trying to say. "We are Pioneer Cops," I finished.

"It's like the Boy Scouts," Popcorn offered.

"Oh! Good for you! But *why* are you here?" Gwen wanted to know.

"Oh, um . . ." I tried once again to project confidence. "We caught some guys trying to use counterfeit money, and the Number One Fan Foundation wanted to reward us," I said weakly.

I was afraid Gwen would say *Hey! That's the plot of* Coyote Willis: Pioneer Cop!

But she just said, "Oh, isn't that wonderful."

The director was still on the stage talking about the

179

Number One Fan Foundation and how it was important to help kids and people and blah blah blah. Then she called Granny Janet to come up and receive her award. I turned around and concentrated on my salad so Granny Janet wouldn't spot me in the crowd. After Granny Janet's speech, Louisa came up to the stage as Mr. Jiggly Fluff and presented a giant check from the Fluff Cream Dairy Dessert Shop to the Number One Fan Foundation. Everyone clapped.

After Louisa/Mr. Jiggly Fluff left the stage, the Number One Fan Foundation director said, "And now, ladies and gentlemen, the man who needs no introduction, whom we are proud to claim as a friend of Haselton: Mr. Tito the Bonecrusher!"

People started clapping like crazy.

"Wooooo!" Popcorn hollered beside me.

Tito was wearing a gray suit and a green-and-red tie that matched his mask. He talked about how happy he was to be in Haselton, the hometown of his best friend, The Germ. His voice sounded exactly the same as in his movies. But he was calmer, probably because he was talking to a room full of rich people and not evildoers like Senator Corruptron. Popcorn didn't take a single bite the whole time Tito was talking. People clapped like crazy again when Tito finished and walked offstage.

The next part of the meal was some kind of meat that had a bunch of long, skinny bones sticking out of it. I saw Popcorn's eyes get really wide when the waiter put it in front of him.

"How do we eat this?" he whispered to me.

"I'm not sure," I whispered back. "Let's just take a couple of bites and then eat the carrots on the side."

We started to cut into our meat.

"Don't you just love lamb?" Gwen asked, smiling at Popcorn.

Lamb? The meat was lamb? Why can't rich people just eat hot dogs?

"Oh, yes," Popcorn said to Gwen, but he immediately stopped cutting the meat and stuck his fork into a carrot instead.

My earpiece started to crackle again.

"I just *CHCHCH* security *CH* Tito is *CHCHCH* during dessert."

Once again I understood only about half of what Brain was saying. I guessed maybe it was that Tito would be signing autographs or taking pictures during dessert.

The lamb at dinner might have been confusing, but the dessert was delicious. It was some kind of chocolate pudding in a little cup with a strawberry on top. The little cup was on a little plate, and the plate was decorated with squiggles of berry sauce and chocolate sauce.

"Yum," Popcorn said when they put it in front of him. Then he turned to me and whispered, "Why did they put the sauce on the plate instead of on the chocolate pudding?"

"I think it's supposed to be fancier this way," I whispered back, and took a giant spoonful of pudding.

Suddenly, Brain's voice was booming in my ear so loudly that I winced.

"*CHCHCH* leaving NOW!" she was shouting. "They just pulled up the car for him. I repeat, Tito is *CHCH-CHCH* NOW!"

I must have looked really panicked. Popcorn dropped his spoon, which clanged against the little plate.

"What's wrong?" he asked.

"He's leaving now!" I said. "Brain said Tito is leaving right now."

"Already?" Popcorn cried. He jumped from his seat and headed toward the front of the ballroom.

I could see Gwen gearing up to ask more questions, but there was no time left for me to project confidence.

"'Scuse us," I said to table 17 as I ran to catch up with Popcorn.

As we hurried toward Tito's table, we saw that he was

already out of his seat and almost to the door beside the stage. Even if we started running, there was no way we could catch him in time.

Then Popcorn did something interesting. He closed his eyes, opened his mouth, and YELLED.

"TITO!!!!!"

Tito stopped and turned.

"TITO!! IT IS ME, PAUL ROBARDS!!!! I'M YOUR NUMBER ONE FAN!"

The room went silent. Everyone was looking at us. I saw Tito looking as well, but he was so far away that I couldn't see his expression behind his mask. I knew I should holler something, too.

"I need your help!" I croaked. My words were barely loud enough to be heard by the next table.

Then two security guys materialized right in front of us. I couldn't see Tito anymore. All I could see were the uniforms of these two tall guys trying to keep us away from Tito, right when we needed him. I felt that buzzing in my bones, and a bunch of the feelings I had pushed way, way down came roaring up and out of my body in a rush of air and loud noise.

"I NEED YOUR HELP!" I yelled this time.

"We are going to escort you boys to the exit," the taller of the two security guards said in a deep, serious voice.

Everyone stared as the security guys led us by the arm past table 17, past the table where we'd gotten our place cards, toward the front door. I craned my neck around to see if Tito was still standing there watching us, but he was gone.

★ 21 ★

GROUNDED

"I hope you have a ride home," my security guy said to us as he pulled us through the lobby, "because I'm not going to be able to let you back in the hotel."

We were supposed to be riding home with Louisa in the Fluff Cream van, but she wasn't going to be able to leave until the end of the gala. And I didn't want to tell that to the security guy, because then he might figure out that Louisa had snuck us into the gala in the first place.

As soon as we were through the door, I saw Brain sitting on her bench.

"Brain!" I called.

She turned toward us when she heard her name. I watched her face as she took in the fact that Popcorn and I were being escorted out of the hotel by security guys. Brain, like I've said, is practically a genius, so I knew she'd figure out that things hadn't gone exactly well at the gala.

She looked disappointed for a moment, but then, strangely, she started smiling. She casually dropped the Spy Buddy walkie-talkie into the bushes and walked over to us, projecting confidence, like Tito would.

"Oh, kind sirs," she said to the security men, "you have found my brothers! You see, they disappeared inside the hotel, and I feared they might have wandered into the wrong room. A ballroom, perhaps. Our father will be along to pick us up soon. Thank you, gentlemen." She nodded politely. "Now, don't let my silly family ruin your evening. I'll take it from here."

My security guy looked at Popcorn's security guy. Popcorn's security guy shrugged. I wondered for a moment if the security guys would actually leave us with Brain and go back inside the hotel.

They would not.

"Sorry, uh, ma'am," my security officer said to Brain. "We can't release them to you." He looked at Popcorn's security guy again. "We should only release them to a parent. I don't really wanna be responsible for losin' a couple of kids."

"I agree," said the short security guy. "Maybe we should let the police handle it."

"No!" Brain cried. Then she added, more calmly, "That won't be necessary, sirs. Our father will be along in a few minutes, after all. Let me just, uh, call him again to make sure he's on his way." Brain pulled her cell phone out of her pocket and dialed a number. "Hello," she said. "It's Brianna. You know, your *daughter*? I just wanted to make sure you were still on your way to pick us up at the Empire Hotel. On Hedgeworth Avenue. We are by the front entrance with the wonderful security professionals who are keeping us safe until you arrive, *Dad*."

I'm not the genius, but I knew there was no way it was Brain's dad who was picking us up. He was on a business trip to Singapore, and I'm pretty sure you can't get to Hedgeworth Avenue from Singapore in less than a day.

"Our *dad* will be here in a few minutes," Brain told the security guy, smiling with her whole face. When she turned to Popcorn and me, though, her expression looked less like a smile and more like panic.

Just then, a couple of news reporters who had been at the gala came out to talk to us about what had happened inside. But the security guys said that the reporters couldn't talk to us without our parents present.

One of the reporters stuck a microphone in Popcorn's face anyway. "Are you really Tito the Bonecrusher's number one fan? Tell us more about that."

"These kids aren't making any statements to any

newspapers!" I heard a voice shout at the reporters. "You should be ashamed of yourselves, trying to interview minors without their parents' consent. No wonder journalism is in the toilet these days."

"Granny Janet?" I said. At first I couldn't see her around my security guard, but then there was a flash of green and there she was, standing in front of me and looking even meaner than usual.

"Granny Janet, I—"

She held her hand up before I could say anything else. "Oliver, I don't even want to know why you and your friends are here," she said, "and we are certainly not going to talk about it in front of these so-called reporters."

"Are these children with you, ma'am?" my security guy asked Granny Janet.

"They most certainly are not," she said in a huff. Then she turned to me. "Looks like you got yourself into quite a jam," she said. "Did you call your parents?"

"Yes, ma'am," Brain piped up before I could answer. "I think that's, uh, Dad now." She pointed to the headlights of a car heading toward us.

"Good," Granny Janet said. "Then I'm going to finish my dessert." She turned around and went back into the Empire Hotel.

The headlights got brighter until the car was in front

of the hotel, where I could see it was a silver Honda with a dent in the side mirror. Carl's car.

"Brain!" I should have played it cool in front of the security guys, but suddenly this whole situation felt less like a Tito movie and more like a mistake.

"We had to call a parent, Oliver!" Brain cried. "I didn't know who else to call!" I think it was sinking into Brain's head that there was no way to save our operation. We wouldn't get to step three.

"We're going to be grounded," Popcorn said weakly.

Grounded was better than jail. My dad was in jail, and he would have to stay there. Because I hadn't figured out how to help him. Three weeks ago on the couch, when Mom was giving me the bad news, I should've just said, *Oh well, that's disappointing*, and spent the next couple of weeks just watching TV and eating junk food at Brain's house. Then I wouldn't have wasted so much time on a stupid plan that didn't work at all.

I felt the bone-buzzing again, this time around my eyes.

Carl got out of the car and walked over to us. He looked like he had been working in his home office when Brain had called, because he was wearing his usual working outfit: the old T-shirt that had a picture of a guy mowing the lawn on it, and gray sweatpants. He obviously had gotten right in the car when Brain had called, without taking time to comb his hair.

Carl may be mostly a dork, but I had to give him credit—he played it cool in front of the security guys.

"Are you responsible for these kids?" my security guy asked Carl.

"Yes," Carl said.

"And you purchased the tickets these two boys used to enter the Number One Fan Foundation Gala tonight?" Popcorn's security guy asked.

This felt like a trick question. If Carl said, *Yes, I bought their tickets*, he might be responsible for all the trouble we'd caused. But if he said *No, I don't think they had tickets*, then we might be in even bigger trouble with the security guys.

But Carl did something much smarter than just answering yes or no. He managed to change the subject!

That old Carl! "No," he said. "I didn't purchase their tickets. They must have bought them with their own money. They must have saved and saved for them. Did you gentlemen ever save and save for something when you were younger?"

"I saved up once to buy a baseball glove and bat," Popcorn's security guy said with a faraway look on his face. "I mowed lawns."

Carl knew better than to stick around while the security guy was thinking about his baseball glove. He hustled us into the car.

"Thanks, Mr. Wyatt," Brain said once we were squeezed into the back seat, with Popcorn in the middle per usual. "That was really gallant of you."

Carl didn't answer Brain. He was completely silent. It was the first inkling I had that maybe he was actually kind of mad.

"I'm going to take your friends home," Carl said, turning to me, "and then you and I are going to have a conversation."

The look on Carl's face told me it was not going to be a casual conversation. It was not going to start with a question like *Hey, is the inside of the ballroom at the Empire Hotel as amazing as everyone says?* I had a suspicion that the conversation would involve my mom, too, and then probably some yelling.

When we got to Popcorn's house, Popcorn jumped out of the car, mumbled "Thanks for the ride," and bolted for his front door.

But Carl wasn't going to let him off that easy. He turned off the engine. "Let's go in," he said to Brain and me. "I'm going to need you to explain your evening to your friend's father."

Popcorn looked kind of nervous when we came into his house right after him. He was standing in his living room. Mr. Robards was sitting on the couch holding an old-looking book and seeming confused. I guess he was surprised to see that Popcorn was home early from his sleepover at my house.

"Uh, Dad, you remember Brain and Oliver," Popcorn said, gesturing at us. "And this is, uh, Oliver's stepdad," he said.

Carl introduced himself to F. T. Robards, who still looked confused.

"Why don't you tell your dad where you were tonight?" Carl said to Popcorn.

Popcorn took a deep breath. He squinched up his eyes. "I WAS AT THE NUMBER ONE FAN FOUNDATION GALA AT THE EMPIRE HOTEL."

I was getting used to this louder version of Popcorn, but his dad looked taken aback.

"They were trying to meet Tito the Bonecrusher," Carl explained. "So they snuck into an event he was attending."

Mr. Robards flushed. "And did you meet him?" he asked Popcorn.

"Not really," Popcorn replied. "I told him who I was. But then they made us leave." Popcorn flopped down on his couch like someone had pushed him.

"We should . . . go?" Brain said.

Carl and I agreed.

We had just dropped Brain off when Carl got a phone call. I stayed with him in the car, where I could see Brain talking to her mom at the front door.

"He's with me," I heard Carl say. Then there was a pause. "I know," Carl said. "I'm sorry. We're at the Gregorys' house now." I wondered if Carl was in trouble, too. It sounded like maybe he had left home without exactly telling Mom that he was going to pick me up at the Empire Hotel.

Carl ended the call and turned to me. "That was your mother," he said. "She would like for you and me to come home immediately. But first, I think we should make sure Brain's mother knows where she was tonight."

My heart started beating pretty fast.

We went into the Gregorys' living room. By then, Brain had told her mom where we were, but it turned out Brain wasn't going to get into any trouble at all. Her mom said that it would be too upsetting for Brain's dad to find out that she had gone to an event sponsored by Designer Mart, even if all she'd done was sit outside on a bench.

Brain looked at me. We both knew the conversation with her mom had been way easier than the conversation with mine would be.

"See you Monday," I told her.

When we got back to our house, Mom was sitting on the couch with Louisa. Louisa's hair was messed up, maybe from being in the Mr. Jiggly Fluff costume, and she looked like she might have been crying. Could Louisa have actually been worried about me when she couldn't find me after the gala? That old Louisa! Maybe she was a softy after all. My big sister. I walked over with my arms outstretched to give her a hug.

When I got close enough to look at her face, though, she didn't actually have that big-sister-reunion look that I had been hoping for. She looked pretty mad. And her fist was clenched like she was ready to punch me.

"Don't you DARE come near me!" she yelled. "What is wrong with you? First I heard that you got taken out of the gala by security, then I heard that you drove off with some strange man you said was your dad, and then I got home and you weren't here. YOU SHOULD HAVE CALLED ME!" She stood and stomped up the stairs.

I will never, ever understand Louisa.

"Have a seat, Oliver," Mom said in a calm, even voice. "You too, Carl."

"Carl is innocent!" I cried. "Don't divorce him! It was all my fault!"

Mom looked at me strangely. "Oliver," she said, "I'm not going to *divorce* Carl because he picked you up from a hotel without telling me."

"Oh," I said. "Okay." I exhaled. "I'm glad you're not that mad."

"Wrong," Mom said. "I'm extremely mad. And worried. And confused. In fact . . ." Her face was looking less calm. "I need a minute," she said. "Go to your room."

I trudged up the stairs, but instead of going to my room, I walked into Louisa's. For once, her door was open. She was on her bed, just sitting there. She wasn't even messing with her phone. I walked toward her, expecting her to roar *Get out!* before I reached the bed. She didn't, so I sat down.

"I'm sorry I didn't call to tell you what happened to us," I said.

She didn't even yell. She just talked in a normal voice. "Why did you care about meeting Tito so much?" she asked. "I mean, I know you really like him. I do, too. Or I used to, anyway."

"Because . . ." I started to feel hot, like I was going to cry. I spoke fast to push the feeling down. "Because he could tell me how to help Dad. He's the one person who could tell me how to get him out of the correctional center in Florida." I swallowed. "And then Dad could be here for your graduation. As a surprise."

It was over. I had spent three weeks so focused on one thing, to never quit trying, and now it was over. And when I thought about that, it made it harder for me to push the feelings down inside myself than it had been to push my clothes and things down in the hamper. The thing I had forgotten about a hamper is that eventually you can't stuff anything else down inside of it. Especially something as big as the disappointment of not being able to help your own dad.

I started to boo-hoo like a real baby, which was pretty embarrassing, so I buried my face in Louisa's pillow.

A few minutes later, I felt Louisa's bed sink down a little bit as someone else sat on it. I knew it was Mom. She waited for me to get myself together, but as soon as I lifted my head out of the pillow, she started asking questions.

"Okay," she said. "I need you to explain to me. What on earth were you doing at the Empire Hotel?"

I looked at Louisa's bedspread and started bunching some of the fabric between my fingers. "Um," I started, "trying to meet Tito the Bonecrusher."

There was a long pause.

"You mean to tell me," Mom said, "that the whole reason for this awful night is that you were trying to see a cuss-word celebrity?"

Something in the way she said it got to me. Like she really thought I had done it just to meet a famous person.

Oh, man. The feelings were all there. I let the angry ones out first. "I didn't have a choice!"

"Didn't have a *choice*?" Apparently, Mom's angry feelings were all there, too. "You didn't have a choice but to lie, break rules, trick people, and put yourself in danger?"

"IT'S NOT THAT BIG A DEAL!" I yelled.

I didn't mean for the words to come out as loudly as they did, but both Mom and Louisa flinched a little bit. So I took it down a few notches and tried to speak in a calmer voice. "It's not like anyone got hurt. Nothing bad happened."

Mom did not take it down any notches. She was crying, her face red. "You sound like your father," she said. "I don't know what to do with you."

"What do you mean?" I asked, searching her face for something that would explain why she said the words *your father* almost bitterly. But she wasn't looking at me. It was like she wasn't even *talking* to me, even though she was talking *about* me.

"I shouldn't have said that," she said. "But you know what I meant."

"I really don't," I told her.

"She means that you did the same thing Dad did," Louisa said. "Broke rules and said you didn't have any choice."

"What rule did Dad break?" Was this a story from when they were married?

"The LAW," Louisa said. "He broke the law for Walker Stewart."

The room got fuzzy. "What?" I said. "I thought Dad was innocent and his boss just took advantage of him!"

Mom and Louisa looked at each other.

"He wasn't completely innocent," Mom said in this really soft voice, like I was a baby animal she didn't want to frighten. "He knew some of the things he was being asked to do weren't right. But he went along with it so that he wouldn't lose his job."

This couldn't be right. The room felt like it was moving slightly, up and down, like it was on small waves. I put my head back down on Louisa's pillow to try to make it stop.

"Oliver wasn't just trying to see Tito the Bonecrusher,"

Louisa told Mom. "He was trying to talk to him. He thought . . ." Her voice dropped, and I thought she was trying not to laugh at me for having such a stupid plan. "He thought he would learn how to rescue Dad. He was trying to bring him back here for my graduation."

By the time she got to *graduation*, I realized she was sort of crying.

Mom's hand was on my back again. "Oh, Oliver," she said. "I know this has been hard for you. It's been hard for all of us, but it's been especially hard for you and Louisa."

"It hasn't been hard for you—you have Carl," I said, my voice muffled by Louisa's pillow. "And Louisa wouldn't talk to Dad. Nobody cares except me. Not even Dad." I thought about how Dad had taken the plea deal to go to jail. "The only one who wanted him to get out of jail and back to Virginia was me. And he was guilty the whole time. I can't believe he was guilty. I thought . . . I thought he was good." I don't know how much of that last part Mom and Louisa could understand, because I was gulping between every word.

Mom stopped rubbing my back. "Oliver," she said, her voice sounding kind of choky. "Look at me."

I wiped my eyes and nose on Louisa's pillow and sat up a little bit. I turned toward Mom and Louisa. Mom was still crying, but not in a big, loud way like I was. Louisa was back to being kind of stiff.

Mom made me scoot closer, and she put her arm around me. She made me look right at her. "Your dad got caught up in something he shouldn't have. He was so focused on getting back here to you and your sister that he went along with something that was wrong. He made bad choices. And now he's dealing with the consequences of those choices."

My eyes were like faucets at this point, but Mom kept going.

"You have every right to be upset with him, but I hope you know that he would do anything for you and Louisa. You said this isn't hard for me, but it is. It's still hard. How could I not care about the one person who has loved my babies as much as I have since the day they were born?"

Under normal circumstances, both Louisa and I would have objected to being called babies, but I was too far gone to do anything other than keep wiping away the tears pouring off my face.

Then Mom sighed and said, "I should have talked to you both more about everything that was happening."

"What was there to even talk about?" Louisa muttered. "You said we had to accept it. So we're trying. But it just sucks. He still lied to me."

I thought Mom would say more about Dad loving her babies or us needing to take things one day at a time or other mushy junk. But she just hugged us both in silence. We sat like that for a while.

It actually wasn't terrible.

★22★

FLORIDA

Obviously, I was 100 percent grounded.
Louisa was, too, for boxing me up, and sneaking me into
the gala. So basically nothing happened in my life until
the following Saturday, when Louisa and I flew to Florida
to visit Dad.

Uncle Victor met us at the airport.

"Welcome to Florida!" he boomed when he saw us
come through security. He had two oranges in his hand,
and he gave one to Louisa and the other one to me.

On our last trip to Florida, Dad had brought Florida
oranges to us at the airport.

"No thanks," Louisa said to Uncle Victor.

"Those are from your dad," Uncle Victor said.

"I know," Louisa said flatly, handing her orange to me.

Part of me was sad that Louisa didn't want her orange
because it was from Dad, but another part of me was like,
Hey, two oranges.

"These are jail oranges?" I said. I hadn't known there was such a thing. I turned them over to see if there was a sticker on them or something.

"Oh my god, Oliver," Louisa said. "No. It's like, a symbolic gesture."

Uncle Victor thinks my dad is the greatest guy on the planet. Like I said, Uncle Victor was wild as a teenager, but apparently he started getting in serious trouble after his mom got sick and passed away. He was hanging around some rough, shady guys and having problems with the cops. But Uncle Victor says my dad helped him turn things around. He even talks to groups of kids about staying out of trouble and not messing up their lives.

It's kind of weird that Dad is the one who is locked up in the correctional center, since Uncle Victor was the troublemaker for so long. But that's how it is, I guess.

"Thanks," I told Uncle Victor. I handed him the two packets of pretzels the lady next to me on the plane gave me because I was "such a well-behaved young man."

"Your dad can't wait to see you," Uncle Victor said as we walked out to the airport parking lot, "and it will take about a half hour to get to the . . . to the place where you'll see him, so we are going straight there instead of going to my apartment first."

Louisa just nodded, and I worked on juggling my carry-on and the oranges.

"So how was your flight?" Uncle Victor asked us once we were in the car.

I guess I was nervous or something about going to the prison, so I started talking and couldn't stop. I told Uncle Victor about the lady next to me on the plane who used to be in the CIA, the flight attendant who gave me extra ginger ale for free, and how I almost lost my boarding pass between the security line and the gate for our flight.

"Would you just shut up for five minutes?" Louisa snapped from the front seat. "How can you feel like running your mouth right now?"

"What are we supposed to do, just sit in total silence?" I responded.

"I'll turn on the radio," Uncle Victor said quickly. "Louisa, you can decide what we listen to."

Louisa started fiddling with the radio buttons, and I sat in the back seat and looked out the window. Everything seems brighter in Florida, I guess because it's so sunny. The sky is bright blue, and the palm trees are bright green. It's like the whole state wants you to feel warm and happy, which is just annoying, especially when you don't feel either of those things.

At a traffic light we pulled up next to another car with two kids in the back seat. The boy was crying and yelling, and the girl was scowling with her arms crossed. I know it's weird, but I was kind of happy to see other people who weren't riding around on bikes and smiling all day, having some great old time in Florida.

We eventually drove up to a pale yellow building with a reddish roof and a sign that said FEDERAL CORRECTIONAL INSTITUTION, SOUTH FLORIDA. It looked exactly like the building Mom had shown us on the internet not long after we found out Dad was going there.

As soon as we walked in, I realized with absolutely one million percent certainty that even if I had met Tito and told him I needed his help, I would never, ever have been able to rescue Dad from this place. The security at the airport was small potatoes in comparison. FCI South Florida had guards, metal detectors, cameras, the works. And there was only one entrance. In Tito's movies, there are always multiple entrances and exits to places, so he can use an entrance where there's only one guard, or the door can be kicked in, or something like that.

Once we got through security, I sat down on a hard plastic chair to wait for Dad. Louisa and Uncle Victor sat on either side of me. I looked at the signs on the waiting room walls. One had a picture of a friendly-looking lady in a business suit, and the text below her photo explained how to get help from a lawyer. Then there were a few signs about the rules.

We sat in those plastic chairs and waited for almost an hour. Finally they called us back to see Dad. Louisa was still crossing her arms. And she took a long time to stand up.

Dad was sitting on one side of a rectangular table in a big room. He looked kind of nervous, like he wasn't sure how we were going to react.

I had planned to be mad at Dad when I saw him. If he tried to hug me, I was going to take a step back, and say something like *Don't you DARE* or *How COULD you?* And then he would apologize for making bad choices and beg us to forgive him.

But when I saw him, I lost track of my plan. I couldn't help myself. I ran right to the table and threw my arms around him like I was four years old.

Dad hugged me tightly, but only for a moment. "We can't hug for too long," he said, glancing at a guard standing nearby. When Dad let go, I thought Louisa would still be standing right inside the door next to Uncle Victor, probably with her arms crossed. But I looked, and she wasn't there.

I looked around the room, trying to figure out where the heck she had gone. This is embarrassing to admit, but

I even bent down to see if she was hiding under a table or something. I don't know what I was thinking.

I looked back at Dad.

"I think she went back to the waiting area," he said gently.

Wow.

"She's really mad," I said. "She . . . Well, she feels like you lied to her."

"I understand," Dad said. "She has every right to feel that way."

Dad paused and just looked at me, like he wanted me to have a chance to say more.

I didn't actually know the details of how Louisa felt, but that didn't stop me. "And she is really confused. She wonders why you told her you were going to be at her graduation when you knew all along you wouldn't be. And she wonders if you are just going to lie all the time."

"I understand," he said again. "I really messed up. I should've known better than to get involved with Walker Stewart."

"Louisa doesn't understand why you did it."

I thought maybe he would say that we were too young to understand, or that it wasn't any of our business, but it almost seemed like Dad had been waiting for me to ask.

"I could tell her my reasons. It doesn't mean they are

good reasons. I thought it wasn't hurting anyone. I thought that doing what Mr. Stewart wanted was the simplest way to get what I wanted, which was to move back to Virginia and get a house with a little more space, and help pay for Louisa's college tuition. But that's no excuse . . ."

I didn't know what to say, so all I said was "Oh."

"To be honest," he continued, "I didn't think about it that much. If I'd stopped to really think about it, it would have been a lot harder to do. And it's the biggest mistake I've ever made. Oliver, there's no way for me to explain how terrible I feel about letting you down."

"You mean Louisa," I said.

"I mean you, too." Dad looked at me. "I'm so lucky to have a son like you."

Here I started kind of crying, which hadn't been part of the plan, either. I wiped my eyes and cleared my throat. "The other thing that . . . Louisa . . . doesn't understand is the plea-deal thing. Why would you choose to go to jail?"

"They were going to send me either way," he said.

"But you could've fought it," I said.

"No," he replied. "They would have gotten me. And who knows for how long, and how much money I would have lost. I'd already had to spend most of my savings on legal fees. I could've been left with nothing and still had to spend a lot of time in jail. It wasn't much of a choice,

Oliver. You have to know that I would never choose to be away from you and your sister if I didn't have to."

I believed him. He looked so sad.

A guard lady told me it was almost time to go.

I squeezed my arms around myself like I was hugging my feelings in.

"I will try to get Louisa to come in tomorrow," I said.

"That's a nice thought," Dad said, "but you don't need to do that."

I hugged Dad goodbye for the day, but I didn't cry or anything. I was already trying to figure out a way to get Louisa into the visiting room with me. As we drove back to Uncle Victor's apartment, in silence this time, I thought about the ways Tito would do it. Maybe I could throw a jacket over her head or something and push her in. Or maybe I could tell her that Bryce from *Los Angeles High* was in the room?

I thought about the signature moves, but none of them seemed like they'd work. I was so disappointed. It had helped me so much to hear Dad talk through everything. I was sure it would help Louisa, too.

Finally, that night, just as I fell asleep, I thought of something I could do.

The second day, the waiting room situation was exactly the same. We went to the prison, waited an hour to see Dad, and they called us back. Louisa stood up slowly, but she looked like maybe she was going to sit right back down.

She glanced at me. I hadn't moved.

"I'm not going," I said.

"Don't you want your time with your father?" Uncle Victor said.

"Yes," I said, "but I got to talk to him alone yesterday. I want Louisa to have a chance to talk to him alone." My voice sounded kind of shaky, but I added, "I'd rather miss some time with him and let Louisa tell him what she really thinks. I know she won't say how mad she is in front of me."

"Go ahead, Oliver, I'm fine," Louisa said. "I can wait out here again."

"Please, Louisa," I said, even shakier but a little louder. "Please let me do this for you. Please go talk to him. I don't care if you yell and scream at him. Just please go."

I hadn't planned to start crying in front of the other people in the waiting room. *Let all your feelings out in public* definitely wasn't one of the signature moves. But as it turned out, the public crying was the move that worked. I think Louisa was so embarrassed to be seen with a bawling kid that she was glad for a chance to get out of there and into the room with Dad. So she went.

Hmm, maybe Brain and I should add that move to the list.

"That must have been hard," Uncle Victor said, "to do that for Louisa."

"Not too hard," I said.

I wasn't sure what to do with the rest of the time. I read all the signs in the waiting room. Then Uncle Victor let me play a game on his phone.

When Louisa came out, her face was kind of puffy, but she didn't look mad.

Even though visiting time was almost up, I was able to go in and talk to Dad for a few minutes.

Afterward, Uncle Victor took us to the beach, which was about 50 percent fun and 50 percent trying not to be annoyed by all the happy families around us.

The third and last day of our visit, Louisa and I both went in. Dad asked us about our trip to the beach, and then he said he wanted to answer any questions we had.

Louisa had a TON of questions about what Dad would do when he got out. She asked where he would work, where he would live, and if it would be hard for him to get a job now that he had a record. He said that because he made a plea bargain with the judge, it would make it easier for him to get a job when he was released. But he looked a little unsure.

"I have some good leads," Dad told us. "I'm lucky to know a lot of people who still trust me. But nothing is certain."

I had been so convinced that I was going to rescue Dad from jail that I hadn't even thought about what his life would be like when he got out. Unlike Louisa, I hadn't thought of any questions, but it didn't matter, because Dad wanted to ask *me* about something.

"Spaghetti-O," Dad said, "your mom said to ask you about what happened last weekend. Something about the Empire Hotel?"

Oh, right. The failed three-step plan.

"It doesn't matter anymore," I mumbled, looking at the table. "I had this plan, but it didn't work." I kicked the heels of my sneakers against the legs of my chair, over and over again. *Kick, kick, kick.* "I tried to . . . find someone to help us. To get you out of here."

It was the first time I had said anything to Dad about the plan to meet Tito.

"What was your plan?" Dad asked.

"Um. Well, we were trying to meet Tito the Bone-crusher. He always knows how to get people out of bad situations, so I thought maybe he could help you. But we didn't get to talk to him. It was just a stupid waste of time," I said to the table.

"It wasn't stupid," Dad said. "You're lucky nothing bad happened, and you absolutely needed to get grounded. But I can think of only one other person who would ever think up a plan so complicated and challenging to try to help me."

"Tito the Bonecrusher?" I said. He was the only real hero, and that was just in the movies and the wrestling ring. I don't know why the rest of us even tried.

"No," Dad said. "Not Tito."

"Who?" I asked.

"Grandma Olivia?" Louisa guessed.

"That's right," Dad said.

Then Dad told us a pretty rough story about why he had to leave school when he was eleven and why he never talks about his dad.

He said that his dad had never been very nice to his mom. At one point, things got really bad and his mom was worried for their safety. But his dad had threatened to hurt her if she tried to leave.

"So she had to make a plan for us to escape," he said.

"She had to plan the whole thing so he wouldn't know. That's how we wound up living with Victor's family."

I knew they'd all lived together, but I had never known exactly why.

"Anyway, your grandma Olivia and Victor's mother, Louise, were two of the strongest people in the world," Dad continued. "And that is why you, Louisa, are named for Louise, and why you, Oliver, are named for Grandma Olivia."

That was a pretty good reason to be named for her, if she took a big secret risk and got herself and Dad out of a bad situation.

"And now *you're* stuck in a bad situation," I said.

Man. This was too much. Louisa was sniffling beside me. I put my head in my hands on the table and tried to pull it together a little bit so I didn't totally lose it like I had in Louisa's bedroom.

"It is pretty bad," Dad agreed. "But I've already served one month of my sentence. I know it feels like a long time, but it could have been much longer. And like I said, when I leave here, I have people who can help me get another job and move on." He glanced around at some of the other people in the correctional center visiting room. "That's not the way it is for everyone."

"I just wish I could have helped you," I said.

"Oliver," Dad said. He almost never calls me Oliver. "You help me every day. Do you know what I keep in my room here?"

"Your clothes?" I guessed. Maybe Dad didn't feel like getting all blubbery and so he was trying to change the subject.

"Yes, my clothes, but something more important," Dad said.

"Hmm," I mused. "Probably your toothbrush?"

"Oh my God, Oliver." Louisa spoke up. "He's talking about something sentimental."

"I have all of Louisa's letters," Dad said.

"I didn't know Louisa wrote you letters," I said.

"I used to," Louisa said. "But not in the past month."

Dad made a little hand motion, like, *Let's not worry about that right now.* "And, Oliver, I have the story you wrote about me in the second grade."

I knew exactly what story Dad was talking about. He used to keep it on display in his apartment like it was a real book. It was called "My Awesome Dad Is Awesome," which I realize now is a pretty bad title for a story. But it was fun to write. I used to kind of like writing, back when I could write about my dad without a bunch of complicated feelings. Now it's just easier to copy Brain's writing.

"Anyway," Dad continued, "I read those letters and that story every day. I don't need Tito the Bonecrusher to know you'd never quit trying to help me. I have never doubted that."

"Oh," I said.

"That's kind of cheesy," Louisa said. "But I guess it's nice."

The prison-guard lady looked at the clock and then at us, and she shifted her weight from one foot to the other. That was the sign that she was going to kick us out any minute.

"It's almost time to go!" I said to Dad. My heart started beating fast for some reason. The room felt kind of airless.

"I know, Oliver." Dad's voice was quiet. "It's going to be okay. It won't exactly be fine, but it will be okay. You can come back down here for another visit next month, when school's out. And we can talk on the phone."

I nodded.

Then Louisa actually put her arm around me, which was weird and surprising. I felt like I could breathe a little bit better. But my head was still buzzing.

"I know," I said. "Okay."

"You're the bravest kids I know," Dad said.

The buzzing got stronger, but I didn't push the feelings down.

The prison guard looked at the clock again. Dad told us to take care of each other. We told Dad we loved him. Then Louisa and I went back to Uncle Victor in the waiting area, and we left FCI South Florida.

★23★

A REGULAR OLD SATURDAY

I'd thought the next weekend would be totally normal—maybe even boring—because it started with a regular old Saturday morning. Louisa was at home, working on her speech (well, her half speech) for graduation. The good news was that Louisa had been named valedictorian, but the less-good news (to Louisa, at least) was that Mitzy Calhoun had, too. They were co-valedictorians, and the principal thought it would be "a fun twist on tradition" if they collaborated on the valedictorian speech.

Meanwhile, I was at Brain's house, stretched out on the couch in her rec room, like most other Saturdays when we weren't starring in commercials or planning to sneak into hotels. The only difference was that Sharon was hanging out with Brain and me again. We had just finished working on our weekend homework when Brain's phone lit up with a call from Popcorn.

"Can you answer it?" Brain asked me. She was teaching Sharon how to play *Coyote Willis: The Video Game*.

"Oliver!" Popcorn said when I answered Brain's phone. He sounded out of breath, like he had been doing jumping jacks or something. "Can you and Brain and Sharon come over to my house? Right now?"

"We're at Brain's house," I told him. "Can you just come over here?"

Popcorn said he really needed us to come to his house. "I have a . . . a thank-you gift for you all. For trying to help me meet Tito."

I glanced at Sharon as she watched Brain play *Coyote Willis*. "Um, okay. I guess we'll be there in a little bit."

"Great! See you soon!" Popcorn said, then hung up.

Brain and Sharon finished their round of the game, and then I played a quick round that ended with Coyote Willis getting captured by the counterfeiters. We turned off the TV, put on our shoes, and walked down the street and up the block to Popcorn's house.

Sharon, Brain, and I climbed the steps to Popcorn's porch. I rang the doorbell.

A large man in a green-and-red mask opened the door.

"No way," Brain said. "No WAY."

There was no way it was the real Tito, even though he sure looked just like the Tito we had seen at the gala and in all his movies.

219

"You must be Paul's friends," the man in the mask said. "Please come in."

It was him. IT WAS TITO. There was no question once we heard his voice. Probably because we had heard it in hours and hours of movies that we had watched and rewatched.

Brain and I were frozen in place.

"Oh my," Brain said. "You're Tito the Bonecrusher."

I'm not proud of this, but I just stood there with my mouth hanging open.

The only one of us to move was Sharon, who curtsied. "I'm Sharon Francesca Dunston," Sharon said primly. "Pleased to meet you. You have a lovely mask." Then she extended her hand to Tito, who had to bend down to shake it.

"Nice to meet you, too," Tito said, then repeated, "Do please come in."

Sharon, Brain, and I followed him into the house. I couldn't stop staring at Tito the Bonecrusher. He had looked big and tall when I saw him from far away at the gala, but up close, in Popcorn's house, he was the most massive dude I had ever seen in my life.

Popcorn and his dad were sitting on the couch, and Popcorn was smiling with his whole face.

"Hi, guys!" he said. "Tito wanted to meet you!"

We stood in Popcorn's living room, gawking at Tito the Bonecrusher. I can't imagine that he was very impressed with us so far.

"Please, have a seat," Popcorn's dad said.

All three of us piled into a huge armchair across from the couch where Popcorn and his dad were sitting. Tito the Bonecrusher grabbed a cookie from a plate on the coffee table and sat down next to Popcorn. There was a long pause.

"I can't believe this! I was just being you," I blurted. "I mean, I was playing you. I mean, I was playing *Coyote Willis*. I mean . . . never mind." My big moment with Tito the Bonecrusher was not going well.

"We're fans of your work, Mr. Bonecrusher," Sharon piped up before I could say anything else. "Yours, too, Mr. Robards," she added.

"Well, I'm a big fan of you three!" Tito said. "And of F.T.'s, too." He gestured at Mr. Robards. "I just read the first few chapters of his new novel, and I think it's coming together well. It reminds me of one of my movies . . ."

Popcorn's dad smiled in a pained way.

"So you really do wear the mask all the time," I said. "Not just in the ring and in your movies and when you know you're being photographed."

"Pretty much always," he said.

"Some people think the mask is silly, but . . . ," I started to say, then stopped, afraid Tito would think the word *silly* was a rude thing to say.

But Tito just nodded a tiny amount, like he wanted me to keep talking.

"But my dad said it gives you strength," I finished. "He—"

"I told him about how we got into the gala!" Popcorn interrupted. It was probably the first time he'd ever interrupted someone in his life. He was beaming. "And how we got kicked out!"

"I heard Paul calling to me as I was leaving the ballroom," Tito explained. "By the time I realized what he was saying, it was too late. The security guards had already taken you away. I made sure to check the guest list so that I could follow up with my number one fan, but there was no one named Paul Robards on it."

"I had to give them aliases," Sharon informed Tito.

Brain was intrigued. "So how did you find Popcorn?"

"My dad!" Popcorn declared, reaching out and patting his dad on the shoulder. "Once I got home and he saw how disappointed I was, he said he thought I should finally meet Tito."

"I read several articles on the surprising benefits of

having larger-than-life heroes in childhood," Mr. Robards began to explain. "And they all said—"

"You had a brilliant plan to meet me!" Tito interrupted cheerfully. "It sounded like the plot of one of my movies."

"A lot of it was Brain's idea," I acknowledged.

"I helped," Sharon said.

I almost added that the whole plan started because we were trying to save my dad, but I didn't. I decided to ask an important question instead. "I need to know something," I said.

"Yes?" Tito looked at me like he was really interested in what I had to say. It was the same look he gives The Germ when The Germ gives him crucial information in movies.

"Well," I began, "if a person was in a federal prison, like maybe someone's dad, would there be any way to rescue him?"

"Oh," Tito said. He looked at Popcorn's father, and then he looked back at me.

I waited for him to answer. It's weird—the whole time I was trying to meet Tito, I really wanted him to say there was a way for me to rescue Dad. But now that I'd missed the chance to help him, I really wanted Tito to say no.

"You know," Tito began, "I'm thinking through all the ideas for how to rescue someone from a federal prison."

"Okay," I said. My heart was beating kind of fast.

"I don't think there is a way that would work. I don't think you can safely rescue someone from a federal prison. Those facilities are very, very secure."

"Yeah, they are," I agreed.

That was all I needed to know about rescuing someone.

After that, we had a million questions about Tito's career. I asked about some of his Arena México stuff. He was impressed that I knew about matches from before I was born.

"I don't know as much as my sister, Louisa, does," I said. "She knows EVERYthing about you."

"Well, tell her to come over!" Tito said.

I called Louisa and told her to come over to Popcorn's house. She said no, and started complaining about me interrupting her speechwriting.

"Put her on speakerphone," Tito said.

Big surprise, when I hit the speaker button, Louisa was still complaining.

"I've only got, like, fifty words so far, and Mitzy said she has three thousand, and I only have another hour—"

"Louisa," Tito said, interrupting her, "this is Tito the Bonecrusher."

"Huh?" Louisa said.

Tito was speaking in the ultimate action-star voice. "This is important, Louisa, so listen carefully. We are eating cookies and there aren't many left. Meet us at Paul's house. Bring the notes for your speech along if you must."

The line went silent.

"I guess she hung up," Brain said.

A few years before, a phone call from Tito, or even his appearance at a gala, would have been the most exciting thing Louisa could imagine. Maybe Louisa really didn't care about wrestling anymore at all, even if she wasn't quite as mad at Dad as she had been before.

There was an awkward silence.

"Would you like another cookie?" Popcorn asked Tito politely.

Just then Louisa came bursting through the door without even knocking. She was breathing hard, like she'd been running. We all turned and stared.

"I decided to come over and say hey," she said, trying to sound casual.

We talked to Tito for a long time. He let us ask a LOT of questions. Well, not really questions, mostly us saying things like "Remember when you wrestled John Rancid in *SummerSmash*? That was so cool," and "Remember when Lance Knightfox rescued his uncle from Senator Corruptron? That was awesome."

Tito told us behind-the-scenes information about everything we brought up, and it was fascinating. For example, none of us knew that he had improvised the line "Looks like you just lost the election . . . forever" when he blasts Senator Corruptron into outer space at the end of the *Time Crusher 2: Out of Time*.

"Do you have any plans for a movie after *Sabertooth*?" Brain asked.

Tito had just finished filming *Sabertooth*, which was about a zoo security guard named Kurt Sabertooth who has to protect a rare, valuable tiger from a gang of animal thieves. There's been a lot of buzz about *Sabertooth* on the internet because it's Tito's first movie with talking animals. We explained all of this to Popcorn's dad, who was not familiar with Tito's complete body of work.

"Well," Tito began, then lowered his voice. "I just signed on for my next project, but it hasn't been made public yet. Can you keep a big secret?"

"Yes!" Brain, Popcorn, and I all hollered.

"I am very discreet," Sharon said.

Even Popcorn's dad looked interested.

Tito smiled. "It's about a man who travels through time to stop some terrible pirates, by any means necessary. Until he learns something that changes everything."

We were silent.

"One of the pirates . . ." He paused.

We leaned forward.

". . . is his great-great-great-grandfather."

"Whoa," Popcorn said. "What's it called?"

"*Captain Dangerbeard*," Tito said. "The script isn't done yet, but the posters are going to say, 'Cross me, hearties, and hope to die.'" He said it in this AMAZING pirate voice.

We clapped.

"We're scheduled to start filming in Florida in a couple of months," Tito added.

"Hey!" Brain cried. "That's where Oliver's dad—" She looked at Louisa and me all panicky.

"It's okay," I said. "Yeah, he lives in Florida. He . . . He's serving time, actually."

"Oh, I am sorry to hear that," Tito said. "That must be hard."

"Yeah. Thanks," I said.

"It sucks," Louisa added.

"Definitely," Tito agreed.

Nobody said anything for a minute.

Finally, Tito said that he and Popcorn's dad needed to talk about some stuff. Maybe they were going to trade writing advice. They went to Popcorn's kitchen, leaving the five of us in the living room.

"Whoa," Brain said. "We were totally just hanging out with Tito the Bonecrusher."

"Yeah," Louisa said as she got up from where she was sitting on the floor. "I bet Mitzy Calhoun's never met anyone that famous."

"She hasn't," Popcorn assured her.

Louisa walked to the front door and put one hand on the knob. Then she turned around and half waved with the other hand.

"See you at home!" I called.

"I have to go to work," she replied. "But maybe I'll bring you some Fluff Cream after work."

Wow.

"What should we do now?" I asked after the door closed behind Louisa.

Sharon climbed out of the armchair and moved to the couch, where she sat primly next to Popcorn. "We could just talk," she suggested.

We talked about school, about what we were planning to do for the summer, and about whether the Wrath of Blanky legends were true. Then we talked about how amazing it was that Tito had said our plan sounded like the plot of one of his movies.

Sharon asked me about visiting my dad. I said I'd only talk about it if she wouldn't make sad faces or say anything depressing, and Sharon said she would try. I told her that Louisa and I were going to visit Dad next month.

"What if you're in Florida at the same time as Tito? Maybe you'll see him!" Popcorn exclaimed. "Maybe you can be in the movie!"

"Hmm," Brain said. "Maybe we can all be in the movie."

"It's in Flo-ri-da," Sharon reminded Brain. "We can't go to Florida. Our parents would never let us."

"I know that," Brain said. "But I have an idea." She grabbed a piece of paper from Popcorn's end table and began writing, ignoring the rest of us. That was typical Brain, to just start scribbling all her thoughts until they were out of her head.

"What are you doing?" Sharon jumped up from the couch. "We can't go to Florida to be in a movie, Brain! My parents won't even let me go to the mall by myself!" She tried to peer at Brain's paper, which just made Brain hunch over it more.

"Jeez, be patient, Sharon," I said. That was just like Sharon to start asking questions before a person had a second to think. "Let's just see what the plan is."

"Fine," Sharon said. She stopped craning her neck over Brain's paper, but she still looked nervous as she sat back on the couch next to Popcorn.

"It's gonna be a good plan," Popcorn reassured Sharon.

"It is," I agreed. Even if our plans didn't work out perfectly, at least they were interesting. They made it feel like we were really doing stuff, rather than waiting around for stuff to happen to us.

Brain scribbled some more, then threw down her pencil. "I've worked it all out," she declared. "We need all the signature moves for this one, plus two thousand dollars. And one of us has to learn how to drive."

"Sounds good," Popcorn said.

"What the heck are the signature moves?" Sharon asked.

"Don't worry," I told her. "We'll teach you."

★ ACKNOWLEDGMENTS ★

Grace Kendall, thank you for your editing brilliance, for making me a better writer, and for dancing with Charlie outside your office. And importantly, thank you for cookies.

Thank you to everyone at FSG who devoted their time, talent, and energy to bringing *Tito* to readers— thank you to Joy Peskin, Andrew Arnold, Aimee Fleck, Nicholas Henderson, Elizabeth Lee, Kelsey Marrujo, Jennifer Sale, Lindsay Wagner, and Janet Renard.

Thank you to Lara Perkins. Who is Lara Perkins, you ask? She is a guiding light, a saint, and a supreme-genius queen wordsmith. She believed in this book for a long time. (She is my agent.)

Thank you to my parents, Mark and Linda de Castrique, and my sister, Lindsay Vivian, who were among my earliest readers (of this book, in particular, but also of some weird stuff when I was really little).

Thank you to the rest of my family—Millie and JP Thomson; Jordan Vivian; my extended family-in-law; my aunts and uncles; my first cousins; my second cousins; my double second cousins; my double second cousins once removed; and my double third cousins.

My favorite memories of Janine Kelker were quite helpful when writing about best friends who co-mastermind some harmless-but-ill-advised schemes. That's all I'll say about that. I miss her very much.

Thank you to everyone who supported this book and/or me along the way—Mark and Kelly Jones; Scott Buchanan; the Roques; Kelly Lundgren; Courtney and Seth Pruitt; Jen Vincent; all my beloved friends from Ramsay; Jessica Beaver; Erin Jeffords; Cooper Drangmeister, my plus-one for Smackdown; Brendan Reichs, *submarine noises*; Laura and Eli Terry; former students who read early pages; all the Chickens; friends who offered virtual encouragement on social media; and literally so many other people. If anyone who is reading this was mean to me as a kid, I just want you to know that I have like a hundred friends now.

Emily Plumlee gets her own line and, at the risk of alienating half of Alabama, a loud WAR EAGLE.

Last but first and always, Pete and Charlie Thomson. I am so lucky that it doesn't even make sense. I love you.